Taboo Explicit Short Sex Stories Collection:

*Erotica For Women-
Threesomes, Cuckold,
MILFs, Hard Anal, Bi-
Curious, Femdom, Hot
Wives, BDSM, Spanking,
69& Orgasmic Oral& More*

Written By:

G.G. Goode

Goode Publications

Table of Contents

Chapter 1

M/F, Newly Single and Wildly Exploring Another Side

As I stood there, in the middle of my new apartment, I dumped the box on the ground and planted my hands on my hips. Well, there I was, ready to take on the world. Even if I had no idea what the world might have wanted from me right now.

I couldn't believe I had finally done it. Finally dumped Ron for good. When I had first met him, back at the tail end of college, I had known at once that he was everything that my family had ever wanted for me – rich, handsome, charming, all of the above. Oh, and he just so happened to be a raging asshole on top of all of that, too, but I didn't mention that part to them. Or to anyone.

But when we got engaged, I started to feel that creeping dread that I was doing the wrong thing. That sureness that I didn't want to be tied to this guy for the rest of my life. He had been my first real relationship – I wouldn't go as far as to call it love, because it had never felt that way to me, not a chance in hell. But I had lost my virginity to him, and I had soon learned that, even if you had never slept with anyone before, you could tell when it wasn't right.

And I knew it was never right with us. Never had been, never would be. After I'd graduated, and as the wedding day drew closer and closer like a meteor thundering towards my life, I kept on trying to find excuses to stay. I knew that my family loved him and loved what he could do for me – he was high society, the way that none of us had ever been before, and if I married him, we'd be front and center to get where we had always dreamed of being.

But that didn't mean that I was willing to go through with it. With any of it. And, finally, just two weeks ago, I broke the news to him that there was no way in hell I could ever marry his crusty ass.

Oh, it was a whole *thing.* My family was furious, his family were furious, he was furious. Even my friends were baffled as to why I had left him. I had always told them that things had been going great between us, even when it was a filthy lie. I just couldn't face up to the truth of what I was hiding, even when I knew that I should. But I was free – finally free, free of the man that I felt like I had been lumbered with these last few years. And I was going to live the life I'd always dreamed of.

And that started right here. With my own apartment. The very first place of my own that I'd ever had in my life. Nobody else to share it with, no other messes to clean up after – just me.

And nobody to keep an eye on who I was bringing in and out of here, either. I had lived with my parents till college, and they had been determined that I would stay away from boys for as long as it took me to get into a high-class college that suited them; I had pretty much been a social pariah, and I didn't blame anyone for treating me like one, either.

When I got to college, I had been so nervous about meeting boys that I had practically squirrelled myself away in my dorm room. Good for the grades, not so good for the ego. After that, I had started to go out with my friends. Or rather, they had coaxed me into leaving the house with them. And that's how I eventually came across him, Ron, for the very first time.

But that whole time, I was still human. I still found myself intrigued by sex, by everything that people got up to in the privacy of their own bedrooms and everything that they did outside of them, too. I knew that Ron was always going to be a lights-off-missionary kind of guy, and honestly, the thought of putting up with that for the rest of my life was enough to make my toes curl. And not in the good way.

And that was what I planned to put right with my new place. Go out there, into the world, and show it and everyone else that I, Jaida, was finally here and was finally ready to find out all the crazy stuff that I enjoyed when it came to sex and sexuality. Yes, I could hardly wait to find out how much I had going for me. And it started right here, with this apartment, with a place of my own that I could bring anyone at all back to that I wanted. I knew it was going to be a hell of a lot of fun. And I couldn't wait to see how far I could take everything.

"Those are the last of the boxes up," The mover, Jason, told me, as he leaned in the doorway. Maybe it was just the excitement of finally being here with him right now, but there was a fizz of a thrill in my belly as I turned to face him; his gray shirt had ridden up a couple of inches, showing off a strip of his strong abs beneath, and it took everything I had not to go sidling up to him and nuzzle myself against his strong chest.

"Yeah, thanks," I replied. I didn't have a lot to my name; Ron and I had lived together for two whole years, but most of the crap in our apartment had belonged to him. Almost as though I had always been looking for a way out and had finally just been handed it.

"You need help with anything else?" He asked me. His eyes lingered on me for a moment, and I felt a little heat rush up my neck. Was he thinking what I thought he was? And was I going to go along with it?

Well, I had to start somewhere. And if this man really wanted to take it to that place...I sure as hell wasn't going to argue with him.

"Well, maybe," I replied, flipping my hair over one shoulder and taking a step towards him. I wasn't sure what it was about him, about the way he looked at me; maybe it was just because I knew I was finally free and could finally do anything and everything that I wanted to do. But I was attracted to him, attracted to him in a way that I couldn't imagine being attracted to anyone else right now.

And I was going to do something about it.

"Oh, yeah?" He remarked, cocking an eyebrow. I didn't even know his last name. I didn't need to. I took a step towards him. He must have been able to see in my eyes what was going through my head in that moment, and he stood his ground. It was strange to think that someone could want me, could really want me like this, but I needed to know that I was capable of taking what I wanted when it was right there in front of me. And that started right here, right now.

"Yeah, I need some help unpacking something in the bedroom," I replied, and I tilted my head towards the space that was going to be my room – I hadn't so much as put a mattress out there yet, but that didn't matter. All that mattered was that I got him far enough into the apartment that my new neighbors wouldn't be able to hear what we were getting up to. I didn't want them judging me before I'd had a chance to introduce myself.

"Sure thing," he replied, enthusiastically, and it was obvious that he was intrigued as to where this was going. How many times had he shot his shot, I wondered, and been left in the dust? Well, I was a single woman now, and I wanted to make the most of it.

I made sure to sway my hips pointedly from left to right as I moved, taking my time, feeling his eyes on my body as I went – it was a hot day in New York, and I was wearing a pair of shorts and a crop top, way more revealing than anything Ron would ever had let me put on.

Not that I was thinking about him right now. Not that I was going to think about him ever again. Once I was into the bedroom, I turned to face Jason again, and I noticed the way his eyes lingered on my body. I loved the way it felt to be the center of his attention like this, loved the way it felt to be the focus of everything for him right now. I tossed my hair over one shoulder and allowed him to draw close to me, my heart pounding so fast in my chest that I was sure he would be able to hear it from where he was standing.

"So," he murmured, his body mere inches from mine.

"So," I murmured right back, and I arched my back so that we were even nearer than before. My flesh was aching now, and I needed to feel him against me, needed to feel him touch me the way I had been craving all this time. I couldn't remember the last time my whole body felt as though it was on fire for anyone; I couldn't remember the last time I had craved, so desperately, the touch of another human being.

And, slowly, he raised his hand and let it rest on my hip, testing me, making sure that this was something I could take. I gasped, my lips parting, unable to hold in the desire any longer – and with that, he leaned forward, and pushed his tongue into my mouth for the first time.

I swear, my whole body sank against his like I was in a dead faint. I had never known the meaning of the word *swoon* before that moment, but the second he touched me, it became abundantly clear just what it meant and how it felt. His cock was already stirring to hardness beneath his jeans, and I pushed my hand up underneath his tee, feeling his strong muscles underneath his skin. His body was so new to me, so new and so exciting – so fucking hot, his hands moving to my ass to press me against him properly as his tongue roamed my mouth.

I had never been kissed like this before in my life, never been kissed like their whole life depended on it. His body was hard, strong, powerful, and he spun me around to push me against the door a moment later. His hands moved over me, across my waist, groping at my tits, down to my stomach and my thighs, as though he was determined to feel as much of me as was humanly possible before this was over.

He hitched me up off the ground, lifting me with ease, and slammed me back against the door; I wrapped my legs around him, unable to hold in a helpless little moan of want as I felt his rock-hard cock grinding against me through his jeans. I needed to feel him inside of me. Holy shit, I needed it so badly I couldn't think straight. I had to tell him, somehow, let him know that I wanted him, but I didn't know how to put it into words. I had never learned to talk something like this into being, but I was going to need to start soon if I was going to become the sex-vixen that I had always wanted to be.

I grabbed one of his hands, guided it to my shorts, and pushed it beneath the waistline; he took my guidance, moving his fingers beneath my flimsy cotton panties until they were against my pussy. His hand was rough, callused, but he could feel how wet I was, how much I wanted him and how badly I needed this.

"Condom?" He murmured into my ear. I reached into one of the boxes that I had dumped in here, and grabbed the brand-new packet that I had made a point of purchasing the moment I had gotten the lease on this place. I pulled one out and pushed it into his hand, and watched as he unzipped his pants and rolled the condom down over his cock. He was big, bigger than Ron, which meant that he was bigger than any other guy I had been with before. This made me more than a little nervous, but I calmed myself down. I could handle this. I could handle anything. I could take everything that the world threw at me. Especially when it was attached to a man as undeniably gorgeous as this one.

I wriggled out of my shorts a little, pushing them down my hips, and he ripped off my panties as though they were nothing more than a distraction in the way of what he wanted to get to. My legs spread, wrapped around him, finally I felt him pushing inside of me – and I let my head fall back against the door as the rush of pleasure coursed through me once and for all.

"Oh, fuck," I groaned, and he turned his head to kiss me again. This time, his tongue was hungrier than before, traversing my mouth like he was starving for me and wanted nothing more than to make sure that I knew it. He started to pound my pussy, going in hard and fast, driving himself into me in long strokes that made my whole body tremble. His lips traced down, over my chin, towards my neck, his teeth baring against my skin as though he wanted to take a bite out of me. I knew how he felt. My mind had all but switched off, the only thing that I was capable of wrapping my head around right now was the pressure of his cock spreading me open for the very first time.

He grabbed hold of my hips to keep me in place as he slammed into me. The sound of our flesh coming together, over and over again, filled the room around us, until I could do nothing but close my eyes and let the sensation flood through me. I could already feel my wetness slithering down the inside of my legs and I knew that it wouldn't be long until I reached my orgasm – I had always been easy to make come, even if my ex had never been able to work that out.

I wrapped my arms around him and buried my face into his shoulder, feeling his muscles moving as he filled me over and over again with his cock. My legs were trembling, the insides of my thighs twitching as he took me, and I groaned again, my breath catching in the back of my throat, as, finally, at last...

"Oh!" I cried out, letting the sound tear out of me before I could stop it – I knew that the people who lived in the apartments around me must have been able to hear everything that was going on in here right now, but I was finding it hard to care. All that mattered to me was the way my pussy was clenching around his length, the way he stilled inside of me as though the pleasure of it was too much for him to take. I was breathing hard, the pressure flooding out to each and every one of my nerve-endings until I couldn't think or see straight.

It didn't take long until I felt his cock twitch inside of me, the pleasure growing too much for him to take, and he came, hard, letting out something that sounded like a growl as he finished. I buried my face into his neck and breathed in his deliciously masculine scent, and wondered how the hell I had been able to go so long without giving myself over to someone like this before. It felt like my whole system was lighting up, my body responding to him in the way I had always known that it should, that it would, when I found the right person to make that happen.

"Fuck, you feel so good," he moaned, as he grinded himself inside me a couple more times before pulling out. He gently lowered me back down again, and I tried to plant my feet on the floor, but my legs were so shaky it seemed a miracle that I was able to stand upright. I leaned against the door behind me for support, and smiled at him, still catching my breath.

"Thanks," I replied, and he pulled me towards him and kissed me again. He liked me. He really, really liked me. He wanted me, and it had been a long time since I could remember being wanted by anyone at all, feeling that desire coursing through his body and into mine.

And I could already tell that this was going to be an addiction for me. I could already tell that this was everything that I had been waiting for this entire time. My whole system was responding to him the way that I had always dreamed that it would, and this was just the start – he was just the start.

And I was sure that I had plenty more to go before I got to the end of this journey that I was only just beginning. Plenty more men to be with. Plenty more pleasure to experience.

And frankly, I was more than ready to find out just how
that would go.

Chapter 2

M/F/F, Threesome, Hot wife, MILF, 69

I hummed to myself as I arranged my knick-knacks on my newly constructed bookcase; okay, so it looked like it was about to collapse in on itself at any moment, but it was standing, and I would take it.

I was finally almost done with the set-up of this place, and damn, would I be glad when the whole thing was over. I had been working my ass off to make sure that it was all exactly as I wanted it; after I had waited so long to find a place all of my own, there was no way in hell that I was going to allow it to be anything other than totally and utterly perfect, that was for sure.

I had been tempted to hit up that moving guy again after he had left – he had given me his number, told me that I was more than welcome to call him up if I wanted to since he didn't live too far from here, but I had sworn that I wasn't going to get involved with anyone that soon. This was the single part of my life, and I was going to enjoy every damn moment of it. Not start calling up the first guy that I had sex with and asking him to keep coming over to see me.

I had a party planned for over the weekend, and I was looking forward to inviting around some of my old friends to check out my new place – since I had been the one to dump Ron, I had expected plenty of them to take his side with the break-up and stick around with him, but it seemed like, as with me, most of them couldn't wait to get rid of him. I didn't blame them; he was pretty boring at the best of times, and his work as an accountant had only limited the amount of stuff he had to talk about.

But for now, it was just me in here; I had taken the week off of work down at the café, and I was looking forward to resting up and taking some time to wrap my head around this new status that I was a part of now. The single life. Strange to think that I hadn't been here in nearly four years, since Ron and I had first met. Even before that, when I had technically been single, I hadn't exactly felt like it, because I had always been building myself up to so much as to leave my dorm room without someone by my side. This was the first time that I was going to be single and going to enjoy it. I wanted to look back on this part of my life with fondness, with all the memories that I'd need to get me through those cold nights when I was an old woman and had lost my mojo.

There was a knock on the door, and I abandoned the snow globe where It sat on the shelf and went to answer it, glad for the distraction. Honestly, this whole interior design thing wasn't really my bag. I pulled the door open, and, on the other side, found myself greeted by a couple a little older than me, who were wearing giant, matching smiles. The woman was carrying a basket, which she handed over to me at once, full of food and a few toiletries.

"Uh, hi!" I greeted them. She beamed at me.

"Welcome to the building!" She exclaimed happily. "We're always so glad to have new people in here. What's your name, honey?"

"I'm Jaida," I told her, extending my hand. "How about you?"

"I'm Courtney, and this is Paul," She explained, nodding to her husband. With his dark, messed-up hair, warm smile, and black glasses, he looked like the very cutest kind of nerd.

"It's really nice to meet you," I told them both. "And thank you for this, really. It's way more than I expected."

"Oh, that's just the kind of thing we do around here," she replied, waving her hand as though it was nothing to her at all. "So, is it just you in here? Or are you with your other half, too?"

"No, just me," I replied. "I don't have another half. At least, not anymore."

"Well, that sounds like a story worth hearing," Courtney remarked, tipping her head to the side curiously. Her long, auburn hair tumbled over her shoulder effortlessly, like she was in the middle of a shampoo commercial or something. With her near-glowing green eyes and flawless skin, she could have passed for way younger than she was, but there was something about the air of command around her that gave her away. As though she knew that she was the one in charge here, and wasn't afraid to say it.

"You should come around some time," she suggested. "Have dinner with us. I'm sure we'd like to hear all about it, right, Paul?"

"Right," He agreed. It was the first word he had spoken since she had opened the door, and something about it sent a shiver down my spine. Not that I was going to go wrecking my relationships with my new floor-mates by hitting on their husbands, of course.

"That sounds really nice," I replied, with a smile. It honestly did. I liked the idea of getting to know these people, making this place really feel like my home. I had to start over entirely, and that meant finding new friends as well, didn't it? I was looking forward to that part of it. Looking forward to everything that came with finding out the kind of person I truly was.

"Well, let's say Thursday night," she suggested. "How about it? If it works for you."

"Oh, yeah, sure," I replied. I had honestly thought that they were just being polite, but it was clear they meant it.

"Good," she replied. "We'll see you then, I suppose."

"I suppose you will," I agreed, and there was something about the way that she said that to me that made me wonder if she was flirting with me. And I liked it!

She nodded, and we said our goodbyes and I closed the door behind them. I could feel a little flush in my cheeks, and I wondered what the hell that was about.

But I found myself counting down the days till Thursday, wondering just what it was about them that had me thinking about everything that had happened. The way they had both looked at me, especially her. She seemed to want to sink her fingers into me, into my mind, and I didn't mind the notion of that one little bit.

I had never been attracted to any women. Well, I had never allowed myself to be attracted to them, that was for sure – growing up in my house, with my parents, the notion that I might have been attracted to anyone other than the most straight-laced boys that they approved of was totally, utterly and completely unacceptable.

But I would have been lying if I'd said that I hadn't noticed them a few times in my life. Not as much as I did with men, not even close, but enough that it made a difference. There had been girls in high school, friends that I had grown a little too close with, who I had become a little too interested in and who my parents had rushed to get me away from, as though they knew what was going through my head.

I had never so much as kissed a girl in my life before, though. Never so much as held hands with one. But I would have been lying if I'd said that it had never crossed my mind. And now, with all this freedom to my name, why shouldn't I find out what I had been missing?

I took my time getting ready for the date that I had with them – no, I couldn't call it a date, I was just being friendly with my new neighbors, that was it. But still, I used the toiletries in that little care package that they had brought for me, inhaled the deep, musky scent of the lotion as it sunk into my skin. It didn't seem quite right for just-friends. Almost as though it was meant for something else entirely.

I gathered myself and headed over to their place – she had popped a note under the door giving me the number of their apartment and making sure that I would arrive there when they were ready for me. I couldn't wait. I hovered outside for a moment before I knocked to announce my presence, but, before I could, the door sprang open, and I found myself face-to-face with Courtney.

"Oh, there you are!" she exclaimed. "I was just about to come looking for you."

She leaned towards me and planted kisses on each of my cheeks, the warm, amber-toned scent of her perfume filling my senses.

"Oh, I'm sorry," I told her. "Am I late?"

"Not at all, sweetheart," she replied, smiling at me warmly. "We were just so excited to have you here already. Come into the kitchen, Paul's just getting some wine for us..."

"Good to see you again," Paul greeted me. He was wearing a button-down shirt, with the sleeves rolled up, and I couldn't help but notice how strong his hands were beneath them. Not something that his demeanor would have filled me in on, but hey, I was more than happy to be surprised...

He handed me a glass of red wine, and I took a sip as I looked around the place for the first time; their apartment had to be twice the size of mine, easily, and it was gorgeously well-decorated and just beautifully put-together.

"I love your place," I told them, and Paul draped an arm around his wife's shoulders and smiled.

"Thank you," he replied. "Though I can't take any credit for it."

"Damn right you can't," Courtney shot back, and we all laughed. I was starting to relax; maybe now that a glass of wine was in my hand, I could let go of some of the tension that had been bugging me since I had stepped out of my apartment to come here. I wanted to make sure that they knew how much I appreciated their hospitality.

And just how far I was willing to go to ensure that.

"I designed this place myself," Courtney explained, as I took another sip of the wine, and Paul turned back to tend the stove where something deliciously fragrant was cooking.

"Would you like to see more of it?" She asked, and the way she phrased it, I knew she was talking about more than just the apartment. I nodded at once. Those eyes, pinned on mine, those lips, painted with a deep red – it would have been impossible to turn her down, even if I had wanted to. A desire throbbed inside of me, a desire that I had done my best to ignore for so long now that I had almost forgotten that it existed in the first place. But here it was, as insistent as ever, and I wanted to give in to the way that it made me feel.

She led me around the living room, where she pointed out some small, gorgeous sculptures, made from amber and granite – they looked as though they had been formed by the wash of a wave; soft, delicate and totally unique.

"We picked these up when we were in Italy," she explained, running her perfectly manicured fingers over the shapes. I couldn't take my eyes off her hands when she moved them, the way she caressed those sculptures like they could feel each and every touch that she made. I Wondered what it would have felt like to be in their place.

She guided me through to the bedroom, where a giant dark-wood bed was laid out with beautiful deep red covers; it was a far cry from the futon that I was currently sleeping on in my own house right now, but they didn't need to know that, right?

"I love your place," I murmured, as I cast my gaze around the room as a whole – I really meant what I was saying, too. There was something about the way it felt, the deep scent of incense that seemed to permeate every corner, that made my body light up with excitement.

Or maybe it was just because I was in the room alone with her right now. It was only the two of us here. And I couldn't help but wonder if her mind had gone to the same place that mine had right now.

"Thank you," She replied. I could hear it then, hear it in her voice – everything that I had been trying to pretend wasn't there, never had been. I wanted to turn to face her, but I didn't know what the hell I was going to say when I did.

So, when I felt her hands on my hips, it was almost something like relief. I knew that she was in the same place as I was right now – that her mind had strayed to the same delicious place as mine had. I turned to face her, slowly, taking my time, not sure what I was going to say when I finally met her gaze.

But there was nothing to say. Instead of words, she just sank her lips down to mine, and kissed me.

She tasted like wine and wickedness and all kinds of fun. Her hands slid to my face, cupping my chin gently, her nails teasing against my skin and making my stomach churn with excitement. I couldn't believe I was doing this right now. I couldn't believe that I was actually going to go through with this.

She pulled me towards her, her touch more forward than I had expected, but I didn't mind. Her tongue parted my lips and she kissed me, slowly, sensually, like she was trying to taste every part of me. My hand, the one that wasn't still holding the glass of wine, was resting on her hip, and I couldn't believe how good it felt to touch her like this. How good it felt to have her body against mine. Her softness turned me on in ways that I never thought a woman could; I had believed, before this, that all I wanted was the hardness that men could give me, but she was proving me wrong in all the ways that she possibly could.

And I wasn't going to argue with her. Not for an instant.

"Oh, didn't realize you were going to start without me."

A voice came from behind us, and I pulled back at once, turning to face Paul in the doorway; would he be mad that I had just been making out with his wife? My heart was pounding in my chest as I half-expected him to storm towards me and ask me what the fuck I thought I was doing right there in his house, but instead, a smile passed over his face that told me that he was enjoying every second of this.

Courtney reached out her hand for her husband, and he moved towards us. My head was spinning – both of them? Both of them wanted me? I was still wrapping my head around anyone desiring me at all, but both of these gorgeous people wanted me and me alone...yeah, it was a lot for me to get through my head.

But as soon as he lowered his mouth down to my neck, his stubble brushing against my skin, as she kissed me once more, I knew that I had no problem at all with how all of this was going to turn out.

I had never had two people pay attention to me like this before. Let alone a couple as gorgeous as them – I could taste Courtney's lipstick, smudged over my mouth, as she began to kiss down my chin and over my throat, her hands coming to the buttons of my dress as she pulled my clothes right off of me. I hadn't bothered to wear a bra, given that my tits weren't that big, and when I felt her tongue twirl around my nipple, I knew that I had made the right decision.

Then, he was kissing me, pushing me back towards the bed – he was a little rougher than his wife, but I liked that. I liked the way that it made me feel. The contrast between them as he guided me back towards the covers made my whole body light up – I could already feel that flood of wetness between my legs, and I knew that it wouldn't be long till one of them gave me the relief that I needed so badly.

"You know, we've been talking about this since we first saw you move into the building," he murmured into my ear. The thought of it sent a hot shiver down my spine, that he traced with his hand, as she pulled my other nipple into her mouth. I looked down at her, at the lipstick smudged over my breasts, and wondered how the hell I was ever going to top this. I was barely a couple of weeks out of my old relationship, and I had already found something that made my whole heart feel as though it was going to explode. Did it get any better than this? And if it did...how?

"Show me," I breathed back to him. I didn't know how I wanted them to touch me, just knew that I had to feel it – had to feel them all over me, their hands hungry for every inch of my body. I couldn't remember the last time that my brain had been so fogged by desire, but I was more than willing to give in to it, to let it rush through me like this.

"With pleasure," he murmured back, and he guided his wife's head down, down between my legs, down until it was just an inch from my aching pussy. I felt her fingers brush down my hips, hooking around the edges of my panties as she eased them off me. She wasn't like that mover guy I had been with when I had first arrived, rough, hungry and forceful, she was careful, delicate, as though she was enjoying each and every moment of this and didn't want me to forget it.

I watched as he guided her head against my pussy for the first time, as her lacquered lips found my soaking-wet sex – I had no idea how I expected it to feel, but the shock of pleasure as it hit me was nearly more than I could take. Her mouth was warm and hungry for me, and this was clearly far from the first time that she had done something like this. Her touch was electric, every caress of her lips against my clit making my entire body rise from the bed like I was possessed by something that was not myself.

I grasped the covers as he kissed me again, the feeling of his tongue against my lips matched with his wife's between my legs driving me crazy. I arched my back, pushed myself against her, knowing that I needed more, more, more – more than she could give, more than I could take. I moaned against his lips, his hands moving to my breasts, pinching my nipples where she had just been sucking on them. They both wanted me so much, and I had no idea how much more I would be able to handle without exploding and just tipping over the edge the way I longed to...

She sealed her lips around my clit and began to suck softly, swirling her tongue around my swollen nub mercilessly, until the orgasm had started to teeter right on the edge of the release I needed so badly. I gasped, my nerve endings burning with sensation as I waited for it – and waited – and waited.

When it hit me, I buckled back into the bed in a helpless heap, unable to control myself. My legs were trembling, my entire lower body burning with pleasure as she continued to lap at my almost painfully over sensitized nub. Of everything that I had expected from this night, this was at the very bottom of my guesses – and yet, it was everything that I had needed.

She moved back up on top of me, smiling, her lips glistening with my wetness as she brushed her tongue over my neck, my chin, and back into my mouth. She seemed to be enjoying every moment of this, especially the parts where I could barely think straight as the orgasm continued to rock through me.

"Oh, honey," she cooed playfully in my ear, like she could see the way that I was feeling right now. "And we were just getting started..."

And with that, she moved to straddle my face, as she moved her mouth back down to my pussy once more. Her pussy was soaking-wet, smelled sweet and musky, and I couldn't resist extending my tongue and lapping against it for the first time.

Oh, God, she tasted good. As she continued to kiss along the insides of my thighs, the outside of my lips, my clit still pulsing against her mouth, I tried to mimic the way that she moved against my pussy with my tongue. Her husband was behind her, pushing her down on me as she rode my face, as she continued to mercilessly eat me out, filling my mouth with the taste of her pussy and the sweetness of her scent.

And I knew that she was right. We were just getting started.

Chapter 3

M/F, Party in The Bathroom

I woke on the morning of the party, feeling more excited for this than perhaps I had for anything that I could remember in recent memory.

I was pretty sure they called it *getting your mojo back.* That was what it felt like, at least – especially the encounter that I had shared with Courtney and Paul just a couple of nights before. I couldn't believe that it had really happened the way it had, but the three of us had spent the whole night together – pleasuring each other, touching each other, tasting each other, like we were starved of everything else.

And then they had even made me dinner afterwards. We had curled up in their bed and chatted and ate and hung out and – well, it had to be one of the best dates that I had ever been on, if not the very best that I'd ever had the joy of experiencing. They were gentle, caring, took their time, never pushed me to do anything that I wasn't entirely sure of, and I was so grateful for that. Grateful that I'd gotten a chance to experience my first time with a woman in a place that was so safe, so welcoming, so open to exploration.

And now that I had...well, I was pretty sure I could safely say that I was anything but straight now. I had always known it on some level, I supposed, but now, it was even clearer than ever before. Even the mere thought of Courtney with her face between my legs had been enough to drive me crazy, and I knew that it would be far from the last time that I went out of my way to visit my oh-so-welcoming neighbors.

Anyway, I had other things to think about today – a party. All of my friends were coming over to see my new place. And if I was going to convince everyone that my new life was as amazing as I had sworn it would be, that started here.

I climbed out of bed and did my last circuit to make sure that I had everything that I had needed for tonight. All the drinks, all the snacks, all the food, all of everything – the music ready to go, the playlists picked out and refined down to perfection for everyone to have something to enjoy.

There was one person I was looking forward to seeing particularly – and that was Ian. He had been a friend of mine back in my first year of college, and he'd recently moved back to the city after spending a few years living in another state. This just so happened to be the first event that he was going to be attending since his return, and I was seriously counting down the minutes till I got to see him again.

I had crushed *hard* on him when in my first year of college. And the little light stalking I had done on social media had served to remind me just what a cutie he was.

Tall, dark, handsome, all of the above. Though I had been way too nervous to even think about doing anything with him when we had been at college together, I was feeling a whole lot more confident these days, and I planned to make sure that he knew it. I planned to make sure that he could see how much I had missed him...

He had always been a bit of a player back when I had first known him, but I'd be lying if I said that wasn't some of the appeal to seeing him again right now. I had never really gone for bad boys, always convinced that they would break my heart too badly, that they would know how to play the game in a way that I would never be able to wrap my head around. But since my liaisons in the last week or so, I was sure that I had stepped up in the world, at least a little from what I had been when we had last known one another.

He was the one I was most excited to encounter again. I wanted to show him how much I had changed. Maybe *really* show him, if he was willing to take it that far...

Anyway, I wasn't going to let myself get distracted with a boy. Not when I was going to make tonight my grand coming-out as a single woman, one who didn't need a man to keep her company, not a chance in hell.

So, I got myself ready for my first house party, took my time picking out the perfect outfit – jeans and a tee, the kind that looked as though I had just tossed them on for no particular reason, but that I knew looked hot as hell on my body. Honestly, as I got ready, pulled my bouncy brown hair back into a ponytail, I wondered if I would ever be able to see myself as anything other than hot no matter what I did. I figured, as I slicked on some dark lipstick, similar to the color that Courtney had been wearing a couple nights before, that it was all about your state of mind, not how you actually looked. I was the same as I had been before, but now, I was better. Stepped-up. Sexy as hell.

And ready to take on anything that the world threw at me.

My guests started to arrive a little past eight, and I would have been lying if I said I didn't notice and totally enjoy a few of the looks that the guys gave me – even the ones who were with their girlfriends cocked an eyebrow, glanced back at me, as though they were making sure that I was really who they thought I was.

"You look awesome!" Kaylee, my best friend, told me as she rolled through the door, holding a bottle of wine and wearing a huge grin. She gave me a kiss on the cheek and looked around my new place.

"So, this is it, huh?" She remarked. I nodded.

"This is it," I replied, waving my hand around. "The bachelorette pad."

"I love it," she gushed, giving me a hug and squeezing me tight. She had been the one who had totally stuck by me from the moment that I had admitted that I didn't want to keep things going with my ex any longer; I think she had been waiting for the day that I was going to come out of my shell and come clean about what I really wanted, and now that I had, she was totally here for it.

"So, you going to get me a glass for this wine, or what?"
She asked me. But my eyes had already slid back towards
the door, where someone had just come in – none other,
actually, than Ian.

"Give me a second," I told her, and I strutted my way
over to greet him. My heart was pounding double-time
in my chest and I prayed that he couldn't see how
nervous I was right now. I was going to give him every
inch of the confident, cool, calm, collected woman that I
knew I was going to have to be to win him over. I didn't
know if I would ever be able to get him into bed, but hell,
it would be fun trying, right?

"So good to see you again, Ian," I greeted him, and I
leaned in to give him a kiss on the cheek – the kind that
lingered a little longer than it had to, making sure that I
brushed my lips against the very corner of his mouth as
I did so. He still wore the same aftershave as he had all
those years ago, a deep, piney cologne that filled my
senses and made my toes curl with excitement.

"You too," he replied, and he cocked an eyebrow as he
pulled back from me, looked me up and down. "You
look...different than I remember."

"In a good way, I hope," I shot back. He grinned.

"Yes, in a good way," he assured me, with a smile and his
eyes lingering on the generous inch of cleavage showing
above my shirt. I liked the way it made me feel, to have
him look at me like that – I knew that, back in the day,
he likely wouldn't have even bothered to glance in my

direction twice, but here, now, I was the only thing that he could pay attention to.

"I'm going to grab a drink," I told him. "You want anything?"

"A beer would be great," he replied. He seemed a little shell-shocked by my attitude – good, that was just how I liked it. I loved the way it made me feel, the control that coursed through me when he looked at me like that. As though he couldn't believe what he was gazing at right now.

As soon as I reached the small kitchen area, Kaylee pounced on me, her eyes wide, and her head cocked to the side with curiosity.

"Okay, what the hell was that?" She demanded.

"What was what?" I asked her, playing innocently, as I went to grab a beer from the fridge for him.

"You were totally flirting with Ian," she pointed out. I shrugged.

"So, what if I was?" I replied, grinning back at her. "This is meant to be a bachelorette pad, isn't it?"

"Wait, I didn't realize you were going to take it that far," she replied, shaking her head at me in shock. "You really...you're really doing all of that?"

"Looks like it," I replied, and she burst out laughing, shaking her head.

"Well, I never thought I'd see the day," she remarked, brushing her hair out of her face. "You're going to become a regular little sex kitten, aren't you?"

"That's the idea," I agreed, tossing my hair over one shoulder demonstratively. I couldn't wait to tell her about everything else that I had been up to since I had moved in here – if she thought this was crazy, wait until I caught her up on the rest of it.

"But if you'll excuse me, I have guests to take care of," I told her with a wink, and with that, I swept off to bring the beer back to Ian.

"So, this place is all yours, then?" He asked me, as I handed it to him.

"It sure is."

"Last I heard you were dating that Ron guy..."

"Oh, he's in the past now," I replied, waving my hand.

"I can imagine," he replied. "I knew it was wrong. I can't picture him with someone like...this."

I laughed. I knew that had to be a good thing. I could feel the way he was looking at me right now, as though he couldn't believe what he was seeing. That was what I wanted from him. That was what I wanted from everyone. That focus, that attention all on me and me alone. I was the one in charge here, I had always been the one in charge. They just needed to catch up with me and figure it out.

I made my way around the room, glad that so many people had showed up – the place wasn't huge, so with twenty or so people there, it felt as full as any throbbing club on a Saturday night. It was strange, I had never really been the popular chick, but tonight, I felt like it. People were coming up to talk to me, to say hi, to tell me how much they liked my place, and I knew that I would turn this into the ground-zero for all the fun that my friends could have. I wanted this to be the go-to place, where they turned when they knew they were ready to have a seriously good time.

And, as I kept everyone entertained, I could feel Ian's eyes on me. A couple of other girls tried chatting him up – I knew that I was far from the only one from back in the day who had felt that lingering attraction to him – but he brushed them off, kept coming back to me, trying to steal a moment of my time wherever he could get it. And I knew that I had him right where I wanted him.

He found me once things were in the groove, and I was taking a break in the kitchen, sipping on a glass of wine and just chilling out. I knew that I didn't need to go over there and beg for his attention – it was all focused on me, anyway. That's the only thing that mattered.

"You throw a good party," He remarked, as he leaned up against the wall beside me.

"I know," I replied, and he laughed. He had a nice laugh – it lit up his gray eyes, showed off the angular features of his handsome face. He had cropped his hair really short since the last time that I had seen him, and he was one of the few guys who had the kind of face that could pull that off.

"Cocky, huh?" He asked. "Not something I expected from you."

"There's a lot that you didn't expect from me," I replied. "People can change a whole lot, you know."

"Oh, I believe it," he replied. His eyes were fixed to mine, and there was something almost more unbearably hot about that than there was about the way they had traced down my body earlier. I kept my gaze steady for as long as I could, but eventually, I had to pull them away. I could feel a heat between us, a chemistry, and I knew that I wasn't going to be able to contain it for much longer. I longed for him. I could feel my body, in its tipsy wisdom, shifting towards him.

"You want me to show you?" I asked him. I could hardly believe what I was doing right now, but I wasn't going to stop. Not for anything. Not when he was looking at me like that, and not when I was able to give him everything that he wanted.

"Show me what?" He asked, leaning towards me, eyes glittering with excitement. And, peering over his shoulder, making sure that nobody was looking in our direction, I decided that it was only fair to show him.

And so, I reached my hand out, and slid it over his package.

His eyes widened as soon as I touched him. He hadn't been expecting that, had he? But if there was one thing that the last few days had taught me, it was that there was nothing wrong with making sure that everyone knew just what you wanted – and that everyone was on the same page about how to get it.

"Come to the bathroom, and I'll show you," I whispered to him, flicking my tongue out theatrically over my lips. God, the way he was looking at me right now, as though he could hardly believe that I was real – this was what I wanted, this was what I lived for. The power that coursed through me when I knew that someone wanted me. Especially someone like him, someone who, in a million years, I would never have thought could even look twice at a woman like me.

He didn't move for a moment, clearly too much in shock to wrap his head around what was going on. And so, I pulled my hand back from his swiftly-hardening cock, and sashayed away from him, towards the bathroom – I shot a look over my shoulder as I went, telling him to follow me if he thought that he could handle it.

And, sure enough, I had hardly made it through the door when he followed me in. I knew that everyone would guess what we were up to in here, but I found it hard to give a damn, not when one of my all-time hottest crushes seemed to finally see me for what I really was.

I grabbed him by the collar, pushed the lock over on the door, and pulled him towards me before I could talk myself out of it. As soon as our mouths met, I knew that I was doing the right thing, I knew that I couldn't deny this. I needed to get him out of my system, if I was ever going to be able to move on from my crush. And I was going to do it with style.

He grabbed my hips and pulled me towards him, kissing me hard, his teeth catching on my bottom lip and sending a shock of pain and pleasure through my entire system at once. I ran my hand down the front of his pants, squeezing over his cock just the same way that I had done when we had been back in the kitchen, but this time, I didn't have to worry about anyone else seeing it. He was swollen beneath his pants, and I could already tell that he was thick and hard and ready for me. I scratched my nails over his shoulder and down his back, and felt the way he pushed towards me every time I touched him.

And God, the power I felt in that moment – the power of being wanted by someone that I had never thought would look at me twice, it was impossible to deny. I wanted to show him just what he had been missing. And I wasn't going to be satisfied until I had done just that.

I dropped to my knees in front of him, unzipped his pants, and took his cock into my hand. He was as big as I had expected him to be – given that he'd had girls running around after him everywhere he went in college, I knew he had to be packing something impressive. My fingers didn't even meet around it, no matter how hard I tried, and I could see the oozing drop of pre-cum that told me he was ready for this just the same way that I was.

"Fuck," he groaned, as he watched me admire his cock right there on my knees in front of him. I pressed my thighs together, trying to contain the wash of want that took through me as I stroked him up and down a couple of times. I loved the way that he twitched when I touched him, as though he could hardly contain his desire in that instant. I wanted him desperate for me – by the time I took him into my mouth, I wanted him to feel like it was the first time anyone ever had.

I had never been into giving oral sex when I had been with my ex – what was his name again? I swear, it was getting harder and harder to remember these days – but maybe that was because he had acted like it was something he was entitled to. I had never much felt like doing it because the way he approached it, it was as though I didn't have much of a choice – and if I was to deny him what he wanted, then I was being a bitch and he would get into a sulk that wouldn't be improved by anything until I did what he wanted me to do.

But here? Now? Ian was looking down at me as though he couldn't believe that he was being gifted with something so sweet, and the way that made me feel set worlds between my last experience of doing this with this one.

Playfully, I extended my tongue, and lapped at the very tip of his cock – I could taste his pre-cum against my lips, and he groaned loudly, clearly not caring one little bit if anyone heard us.

"Fuck," he growled, and he reached down to wrap my hair around his hand. His grip was firm, but it was clear that he was still leaving me in control right now, ready for me to do anything and everything I wanted to him. I held back for a moment, not quite sure how far I was willing to take this right now. Maybe I would get to my feet and just walk out of here, leaving him with a hard-on wondering how long it was going to be before I came back and gave him what he wanted.

Who was I kidding? I had been waiting far too long for this to hold off now. I planted a wet, sloppy kiss on the head of his cock, and then moved forward to take him into my mouth.

The fullness of his cock as he penetrated my mouth for the first time caught me off-guard. Maybe because I hadn't expected to like it so much, the way that it felt between my lips, or maybe because I had never taken another man into my mouth before this moment. He flexed his hips to push in a little deeper, his entire body tensing as he groaned with pleasure again, and I reached up to grip hold of his thighs, squeezing my fingers into his flesh and reveling in the delicious sensation of him inside of me.

I was going to give him the best damn blowjob of his entire life. That much, I was certain of. I ran my hands down his bare thighs, letting my fingertips trace against his skin, and felt for the way he moved as I touched him. I responded to every motion that he made to me, all the ways that he shifted and bucked to push inside of me, as I softened my mouth around him, running my tongue up the underside of his erection, finding that seam that ran from his balls to his tip.

I pulled back for a moment, suckling on the very tip of his cock, looking up at him with what I hoped passed for innocence in my eyes. His gaze was already a little blurry around the edges, as though he could hardly believe that this was really happening. I knew how he felt. All the times I had dreamed of being with him, it had never looked like this, never looked as rough and as passionate as this did.

But I was a different woman than the one who had existed when I had first fantasized about him – I was a different woman now, and I was going to make sure he knew it. I twirled my tongue around his tip, around the thick mushroom of his head, and then dived forward again to take as much of him into my mouth as I could manage.

His erection hit the back of my throat, so big that I almost gagged on it in shock, but I managed to calm my muscles before I made a fool of myself, pulled myself together – and pushed forward further. I stared up at him as I took his cock deeper and deeper into my mouth, feeling it stretch and push inside of me, the way that it opened my throat to drive itself deep, deeper, deepest.

"Fuck, Jaida," he groaned, and he ran his hand over my head as though he was marveling at the sheer gloriousness of what I was doing for him right now. I pushed deeper, determined to take every inch of him, until my nose was pressed up against his pubic hair. And, even though I knew it was ridiculous, I couldn't help but feel a thrill of achievement when I realized that I had managed to fit his whole length inside of me, just the way I wanted to.

"You look so good like that," he growled, as he tightened his grip on the back of my head and pushed me down a little deeper. My lips were throbbing, spread wide around his cock, but I didn't care – I wanted to show him just what he had been missing this whole time.

The moment that he pulled back from me, I caught my breath, a string of saliva attaching my tongue to the head of his cock. I was downright proud of what I had just done – showed what was possible when I was actually into the sex act that I was performing, right? His eyes were shining down at me, as though he was seeing me for the very first time, and I rolled my tongue around his tip again, almost casually.

"Good?" I asked. I already knew the answer to that question.

"So fucking good," he growled. And with that, he thrust forward once more, and began to fuck my mouth properly for the first time in my entire life.

And fuck, it was hot as hell. To know that I had driven this man, this man who must have had a million women a million different ways over the course of his life, to such helpless arousal that he couldn't even come close to controlling himself – that was what I wanted, what I longed for. I needed him to look deep into my eyes and see that I was the woman that he had been waiting for all this time, that I was the girl that could pleasure him the way no other could. I wanted him to walk out of this party totally and utterly addicted to me, no room for anything or anyone else, and that was precisely what I intended to do.

I grabbed his thighs once more and pulled him deep inside of me, until I could feel his full length down my throat, and allowed him to use my mouth as his toy. I could feel the warm heat spreading between my legs, and I couldn't help but push my hand down to find it, caressing my pussy underneath my panties, the wetness already slick against my fingers.

And it was like that, in that pose, hand between my thighs, that I took him over the edge. As soon as he saw that I was getting myself off to this just as much as I was pleasuring him, any control that he might have been hanging on to just vanished at once, and he let out a deep, throaty groan and came hard, in the same moment that I did.

I didn't pull back from him, not for a moment, allowing the flood of his seed to fill my mouth, taking every drop of it that I could and swallowing its warmth down my throat without a second thought. And I knew, as I watched him catching his breath above me, as I watched him tip his head back and growl with delight, that I had given him something that he was never going to be able to forget. Of all the women that he had been with, of all the girls that he had experienced in his life, I would be the one that he kept on coming back to in his head.

Because he had never expected this from me. And that would endlessly mark it out as a moment to remember.

I rose to my feet, theatrically flicked my tongue over my lips, and smiled at him. My pussy was still throbbing from the orgasm that I had just given myself, and my legs were a little shaky as I went to wash my hands and smooth down my hair.

"That was unbelievable," he murmured, grabbing my hips and pulling me back against him, nuzzling against my neck for a moment. I glanced at the two of us in the mirror and couldn't help but smile at the sight of us together like that. I had never imagined that someone like him would be willing to look twice at someone like me, and here he was, clearly already lusting for more.

But I had a party to attend, and I wasn't about to let him distract me from it. I knew that he would have done just about anything to keep me there with him right now – but honestly, that just made it all the more fun to take a step back and give myself a break. I would leave him wanting more, and surely, it wouldn't take long before he came back to claim it.

"Anyway, I have guests to attend to," I told him, lightly brushing him off of me. He raised his eyebrows. I could tell that he would have done anything at all that I asked him to in order to keep me here with him, but it wasn't going to work. I wasn't going to let that happen. I wasn't the girl who just gave in to any boys who looked at her the right way – no, I was the woman who took what she wanted and got back to her real life. Because I wasn't hung up on any one person in particular, and I wasn't going to let myself get pulled back into that place in my mind again.

"See you back out there," I told him, flashing him a grin, enjoying the amazed look on his face as I did so – as though he could hardly believe that I was really turning down the chance to enjoy more with him. I supposed that not many women had, in his time, but he was going to have to get used to it if he wanted me.

Because I wasn't stuck on anyone right now. I wasn't pinned down to a single person. And I was going to do everything that I could to make sure that I got out into that real world – and showed it just how much it had been missing when I had been tied down.

Chapter 4

F, Solo, Masturbation, Semi-Public

I ran my hand over my hair, patted it back into place, and eyed myself for a moment.

It was the first day that I would be back at work since I had...well, since I had changed everything about myself. And I was, frankly, looking forward to seeing if any of the people I had worked with for the last three years noticed anything different about me.

I wasn't sure if there was anything different to notice, not really. Not on the surface, at least. But they hadn't seen me in a week, and that week had probably been one of the most eventful of my entire life. I didn't want to let anything get in the way of how much I had enjoyed it – and, more than anything, I wanted it to come with the assurance that I was a different person now because of it.

Between my moving day, my dinner with Courtney and Paul, and the party over the weekend, I felt as though I had run the gamut of everything that I had expected to experience when it came to my new sex life. And honestly? It had been so much fun that I wasn't sure I had been totally ready for how much I was going to enjoy it. Spending time with these people, learning about their bodies, watching the way they reacted when I touched them – there was a thrill to that which I was sure I would never grow tired of, and I didn't want to let it slip through my fingers.

Not that I intended to allow that to happen – not for an instant. But I needed to turn around some of the focus to myself, I was sure of that, make sure that I didn't let my own wants and needs get forgotten in all of this. I needed to remember that I was at the top of my to-do list. And now that I was going back to work again, I was going to have to work double-time to make sure that my own wants didn't get forgotten.

I smoothed down my work shirt, and headed out the door to the café. I had been working there since I had left college; my degree had been in English Lit, and, as the old saying went, it turned out that there wasn't much in the way of work for people who only cared about words. Not that I minded – the coffee shop that I had worked at all this time was one of those little hipster-y places, filled with people who seemed to enjoy writing and talking about books and about all their many, many projects that they were definitely actually working on and not just coming down here to try and avoid looking in the eye.

My boss, Helen, was already opening up by the time I got there, and she waved at me as she saw me coming down the street.

"Hey!" She called to me brightly. I didn't know how she always seemed to be able to approach anything and everything with such a warm attitude, but it was a skill that I hoped I might be able to adapt for my own one day.

"Hi," I replied, offering her a smile. I was still a little tired – catching up on my rest from a very busy few days – and I knew that work was only going to strip me of more of my energy.

"How was the move?" She asked me, as she opened the shutters and led the way inside. I nodded.

"It was good," I replied, trying to keep the smirk out of my voice, but she must have heard it anyway.

"Something up?" She asked, and I shook my head at once. The last thing my boss needed to hear about was my many exploits with people I should have known better than to get involved with. Hardly very professional.

"Nothing," I replied, and I hustled my ass over to the coffee machine to switch it on. "Anyway, how have things been here?"

I let her talk away to me, and found myself relaxing into the familiar chatter of this place as the normal slew of customers came through the door. I greeted each and every one of them with a fervor that I had never had before, and I swear, a few of them noticed it. The men, especially.

If there was one thing that I was figuring out about men, it was that they seemed to respond to the barest hint of attention that you headed in their direction. Like they were just holding out for a woman to give them the merest nod, and they would do everything that they could to please her and make her happy. It was a powerful thing, and I intended to make the very most of it.

One of the regulars who had been coming in since I had started working there, Tommy, approached the counter with his usual cocky swagger. He would flirt with whoever was behind the counter, man or woman, but today, he was going to be met with someone who was actually willing to flirt back for a change.

"The usual?" I asked him, already firing up the coffee machine in preparation for his order. He nodded.

"Glad that I made such an impression," he shot back.

"Or maybe you just come here so often that you make it impossible to ignore you," I replied. He laughed. It lit up his whole face — slightly crooked smile, brown eyes, messy, curly dark hair. The kind of hipster dreamboat which many women must have fallen for in his time. Many men, too.

That part of him intrigued me, I had to admit it. I had never really known a man who had so much as held hands with another dude before, and the thought of actually getting to explore that with someone who knew what they were doing in that arena was...interesting, to say the least.

I made him his usual coffee, allowed him to hit me with the usual conversation that he did whenever he came in here. But instead of laughing off his flirtation, I engaged with it, throwing it right back at him in a way that I knew excited him. I could hear it in his voice, that tension, that fascination. He wanted me. God, had it always been this easy to get men to desire me? And I hadn't been making the most of it all this time? It seemed ridiculous now, now that I knew how simple it had been, and I wasn't going to let that slip through my fingers.

"You know, I don't think I've ever seen you outside of this place," he remarked to me.

"I try not to be seen out of here," I joked back. "Makes it easier to keep up the mystique."

"I'd like to find out what's behind it," he replied, leaning back against one of the tables behind him. Wait, was this really happening? Was it that easy?

"How do you mean?"

"How about I take you out sometime, and I show you?" He suggested. I grinned as I finished making his coffee, added the last dusting of cinnamon on top of it and then handed it across to him. Just as I had suspected – easy to get him right where I wanted him.

"Sure thing," I replied, and I pushed the coffee over the counter towards him. He handed me the cash to pay for it, and then pulled out his phone and gave it to me as well.

"Put your number in," he told me, sounding a little shocked that it had worked as easy as that. "I'll call you, okay?"

"Text me," I replied. "I'm going to be at work. I don't want to get distracted."

"Sure, sure," he agreed, and his eyes danced over mine for a moment. I could tell that a number of lewd thoughts were rushing through his head in that instant, and the thought of them, what they might have been, thrilled me.

"Speak to you soon," I told him, and I turned away from the counter again, hoping that he couldn't see the flush to my cheeks as I did so. I couldn't believe that I had been so bold, couldn't believe that I had done something so daring. Couldn't believe that this was really happening to me right now, that I was really living out all the gorgeously sexy fantasies that I'd barely even allowed myself to have when I had been with that boring-ass ex of mine.

Anyway, I tried to stay focused on work, but something about the interaction I'd just had made it impossible to keep my head on what I was meant to be doing right now.

I knew that this kind of power would change me. That I would shift inside myself, move to find a new version of the woman that I had been all this time. But I hadn't expected it to thrill me the way that it did. As I moved around the coffee shop, smiling at the regulars, bantering with the rest of the staff, it was as though I was hiding a small, sultry secret inside of me. A secret that I just wanted to spill to the rest of the world already – a secret that I wanted to make sure everyone understood the meaning of.

But I had to contain it, at least for now, and that was driving me a little crazy. I could feel people looking at me, feel their eyes on me, and it was impossible to deny how much it turned me on.

To the point that I was having a hard time even thinking of anything else. How could I, when this was all that seemed to be playing on my mind right now? By the time my break came around, I had to shut myself in the bathroom to gather myself, trying to find a way to make sense of the flushing floods of desire that coursed through my brain every time I let myself linger on what had happened over the last week or so.

I bolted the door behind me, and leaned against it to catch my breath. God, I was horny right now. I couldn't remember the last time that I'd been dealing with this hormonal flush of want, at least not since I was a teenager, but it seemed as though my brain wasn't going to let me forget about it anytime soon. And maybe I – maybe I wanted that? Maybe I wanted to give in to my base urges right now?

But I was at work. Just outside of that door, there were my colleagues, my customers, my damn boss. If I got caught doing something like this in the bathroom, I would be in so much trouble...

And the thought of that was enough to tell me what I needed to do. I unbuckled my pants, pushed them down an inch or two, and shoved my hand down my panties so that I could find some relief.

"Oh," I groaned, my whole body tensing up as my fingers pressed against my clit. Just like they had done when I had been on the bathroom floor, sucking Ian's cock, a few days ago. The memory of that was blended with the lust that I'd felt coming off Tommy, full-force, and I could almost picture him in front of me now, his hard-on in his hand, begging me to suck him off.

My fingers started to move with more force against my pussy now, and I couldn't help but slide them down, guiding them against my slit. I pushed one inside of me, and gasped, imagining that it was Tommy's cock — imagining him in front of me, begging to fuck me, willing to do anything if it meant that he could pleasure me the way he knew I deserved.

I was breathing hard, my whole body tensed as I fucked myself with my fingers right there in the bathroom at work. I knew that, if anyone so much as knocked on the door, I would be exposed, found out. They would be able to take one look at my face and guess what I had been up to, and honestly, something about that thrilled me even more. Maybe I wanted to be caught, wanted to be exposed, wanted to be found out as the horny little slut that I seemed to have become...

And it was with those words in my mind that I came, hard, against my hand, my whole body shuddering as I found my release once and for all. I groaned, biting down on my lip to keep myself quiet, and hoping that the music they played in the café would be enough to disguise the sounds of my orgasmic pleasure happening right beside them.

I held my hand against my pussy for a moment longer, and then, finally, drew it back, going to wash up quickly before I made my way to the break room for something to eat.

Not that I was hungry. Not for food, anyway. No, there was only one thing on my mind right now, one thing that I wanted to feast on.

And I was waiting for his text as we speak.

Chapter 5

M/M/F, Threesome

I bit my lip as I leaned on the bar, glancing around and wondering how long they were going to keep me waiting.

Tommy and I had planned out this date down to the last detail – honestly, I had been half-expecting him to just back out and tell me that all of this had been nothing but a joke at my expense. Not like he couldn't have found someone to take my place if he had wanted to, and truly, I kept on waiting for that penny to drop.

But it didn't. In fact, when he suggested this fancy bar downtown for us to meet at, it became even more clear how seriously he was taking this. He really wanted to impress me. And I wasn't sure why, but I was still surprised that any man gave enough of a damn about me to make that effort.

I had picked out a dress for the occasion, something flimsy and flirty that would fall off of me at a moment's notice when the time came for us to go to bed. Because Tommy had a hell of a reputation, with men, with women, with pretty much anything that was willing. And I was going to make up that side of it tonight.

There was something else, though, something else that he had peppered into the conversation when we had been organizing this. And that was the other man he was bringing with him. An old college roommate of his, who was in town over that weekend and who wanted to see some of the city. The way he had talked about him, it was clear that it was more than just a friend of his, and I was curious to know why he thought he should bring him along to our first date.

But I would find out soon enough. And I was sure that I was going to like what came of this.

I glanced over my shoulder, and, at last, I spotted Tommy heading through the door. He was wearing jeans and a blazer, with a button-down, casual but cute, and he was looking over his shoulder when he got there, chatting to someone else.

And there he was – the other man. He was a little taller than Tommy, blond, classically handsome in that old-fashioned way, and I would have been lying if I said that there wasn't a part of me that tingles at the thought of getting to enjoy his attention for an evening.

I rose to my feet as they drew closer to me, and Tommy greeted me with a kiss on the cheek – way friendlier than he needed to be, but then, he knew what I wanted from this night, just the same way that he did.

"You look gorgeous," he told me, his gaze drifting up and down my outfit.

"Not so bad yourself," I replied, and I smiled at his friend. "And this must be...?"

"Johnathan," he introduced himself, extending a hand to me with total confidence. Given that he was basically crashing a date, I wondered how he could carry himself with such certainty.

Maybe because he knew that he wasn't crashing at all. Maybe because Tommy had gone out of his way to give him an invite.

"It's so good to meet you," I told him, as my hand rested in his warm grip for a moment. He was confident, that much was obvious, and he carried himself with a cool, calm sureness that made me feel safe at once.

"Drinks?" Tommy suggested, and I nodded.

"Sounds good," I agreed, and I turned back to the bar. Tommy and Johnathan were either side of me, I was pressed right in between them, and I would have been lying if I said that there wasn't a part of me that was thrilled at the thought of being seen out and about with two such gorgeous men.

Tommy insisted on paying for our drinks, and he was able to grab us a table in no time; the place was packed, but it seemed like he had a certain pull here. I wondered just what he had going for him. It was obvious that he oozed confidence, had been from the first day that I had met him, but the rest of the world seemed to respond to it just the way he wanted them to — that was a skill that didn't come quite as easy, I was sure of that.

The drinks were luscious and strong, and it didn't take long till any doubts that I might have been holding on to about this flooded from my mind, to be replaced with the bright, flirty energy that a couple of cocktails could give to a girl. The two guys bounced off each other with confidence, and it was clear that they had known each other a hell of a long time to be able to converse as easily as this. Maybe known each other intimately, too – I noticed the way that they spoke, the way they shifted towards each other on occasion, and it thrilled me to think of the two of them together. You know – *really* together.

"So, how did the two of you meet?" I asked them, leaning forward with interest. I didn't know what I expected to hear in answer to that question, but damn, I was curious. I had never really been around men who had any interest in other men before – in fact, I think my ex and most of the people that he kept around him would have rather cut their dicks off than spend a minute in the company of a dude who might have been attracted to them.

"College," Johnathan replied with a grin, shooting a glance over to Tommy as though recounting all the fun they'd had there. "We were on the same floor together in dorms, and it didn't take long for us to find each other."

"You make it sound like we were dating," Tommy teased him.

"Oh, yeah, it was never like that," Johnathan laughed. "More...casual."

"Like how?" I asked, shifting forward again, lowering my voice to make sure that nobody else could hear me. Honestly, I wanted this just between the two of us. I liked the thought of it just being here, being secret – even though we were in a bar full of people, I wanted to keep all of this to myself.

"Like, I had never been with a guy before," Tommy explained, and I could hear that edge to his voice that told me that this was a hot little memory for him to pull up. "And then I met John, and I – well, I figured out all the ways that I was different from the people that I had grown up with, put it like that."

"Damn, you make it sound like I dragged you out by your collar," Johnathan laughed. "You were the one all over me, remember?"

I could feel the chemistry between them now, and it thrilled me. The thought of them touching each other, the thought of their bodies together – the thought of me between them, with them, getting to experience all of it right alongside them. I had to cross my legs under the table, hoping that they couldn't see how absurdly turned-on I was just from this conversation.

It didn't take long till things took a turn for the – well, for the more interesting. Tommy suggested that we go back to his place for another drink, and I found myself nodding along at once, no idea how to say no, no urgency to do anything but agree, agree, agree.

I wanted to find out what else they had going on under there. If the chemistry that they shared translated to something that might just be able to involve me, if I played my cards right.

Tommy poured us both a drink once we had reached his fancy little apartment downtown, and Johnathan and I sat on the loveseat together. His arm was draped along the back of the couch, lazily lying there like he was trying to hint something that he didn't know how to say. I shifted an inch or two closer to him, wanting this, wanting more, wanting as much as I could manage. I needed to see where this could take me. I needed to find out where this could go.

"Fun night, huh?" He remarked, and I nodded. I felt as though I was going to dive towards him at any moment, lean my body against his and just let this happen. But I didn't want to jump the gun. I didn't want to get in the way of whatever it was that they had here. I knew that the three of us were working our way towards something, and I would be damned if I passed up the chance to see what it was.

I had already been with a man and a woman at the same time. And I wanted to find out what happened when I was with two men at once.

I bit my lip and nodded.

"Really fun," I agreed, and his hand traced over the top of my exposed shoulder. I shivered. I wanted nothing more than to see where he was going to take this next. His touch sent a shockwave through me, and his eyes pinned onto mine, clearly daring me to say something about this. Daring me to do something.

"Have you ever been with two men before?" He asked me. His words were so blunt that they caught me off-guard, but I sure as hell wasn't going to complain. Not when he was looking at me like that, not when the mere sound of those words was enough to make my entire body tense up.

I shook my head. I didn't know how to respond to that with words, not when I could have just let him show me the way.

"We've done this so many times before," he murmured, and his fingers traced over my neck, up to my chin, where he caught it in between his thumb and forefinger. My lips parted. I wanted to feel him kiss me, but the anticipation was almost as sweet as the actual feeling of him going and doing it.

"Have you?" I breathed. "I – I've never..."

But before I could get the words out, he leaned forward, and pressed his lips against mine.

As soon as our mouths met, I found all the questions falling away at once. I knew that none of them mattered, not really, as long as I was just here with him – here with this man who made me feel so alive, who made me feel like my whole body had been built for him. As I heard footsteps, Tommy entered the room once more, I didn't even pull back. If they really knew what they were doing, then this would be simple.

I felt the weight of him beside me, his hand on my leg as Johnathan continued to kiss me, and I swear it took everything I had not to give in to their advances on the spot right there – I could feel my body crying out for them, for the power that these two men could bring to me. I wanted to be with them. I wanted to feel their strength, I wanted that inimitable masculinity to surround me, more than anything in the world.

Tommy's hand came to my face, and he turned it to look at him – he smiled at me for a moment before he kissed me, and the feeling of his lips so soon after John's was so perfect it made my head spin. Johnathan's lips found my neck, soft kisses marking a line down my throat and across my shoulder, his hands pushing down the straps of my dress so that he could go further, further, until his lips had found my nipples.

Tommy pulled back for a moment, looked down, to see what his friend was doing to me. He grinned, and I could see the flush of want in his eyes, the desire that told me I was everything he had needed.

"Fuck, you look hot like that," he murmured, and he pushed his hand through John's hair and held him in place. I had no idea whether he was talking to him or me. I didn't care. All I cared about was feeling the touch of his lips again.

With Johnathan at my breast and Tommy at my lips, it didn't take long for me to settle into the feeling of being at the center of their attention. I wanted to be shared by them, had by them – I wanted to be taken. I knew that I was just another one of the girls that they'd brought into this little set-up that they had, but there was no way that

I was going to argue with that when it felt so fucking good.

Tommy's hand moved to the hem of my dress, and he pulled it up, sliding his hand across my panties so gently that it made me gasp. He glanced down once more, and this time, took his hand to Johnathan's head and pushed it down between my legs.

"Here," he murmured to me. "I know what he's good for..."

Johnathan pulled off my panties as Tommy sank his lips to mine once again, and I groaned as I felt his lips caress my clit for the first time. I was already so wet that I was sure I would soak him, but hey, they would take that as a compliment, wouldn't they? My hips were grinding back against him, loving this, wanting this, needing it. Needing more.

Johnathan really was good at giving head – his tongue swept back and forth across my clit and then circled in around it until my legs were shaking. It reminded me a little of the night that I had spent with my neighbors, but I knew that it was going to take an entirely different path by the time it was done with. I slid my hand down to Tommy's crotch, feeling the hardness of his cock beneath his pants, and I swear it was almost as though I was being drawn by some ridiculous force to feel him inside of me.

"You want me to fuck you?" He asked me, his lips trailing oh-so-lightly over my ear as he spoke. I nodded. I didn't have any other way to put it into words.

"Think you can handle both of us?" He wondered aloud. I bit my lip. I had no idea what that was going to look like, but damn, I was intrigued to find out.

"I think I can try," I replied, and I looked down to see Johnathan peering up at me from between my legs – his lips were smeared with my glistening wetness, and the sight of him like that was almost enough to make me forget what they had just asked me.

But, as Tommy brought me to my feet and guided me to the bedroom, I knew what was to come. These two men – I was going to have both of them at once, and I couldn't think of anything in the world more exciting than that right now.

It was different to the way it had been when I had experienced my very first threesome – there was something harder about them, more passionate, and I was already finding myself well and truly addicted to it. As Tommy pushed me down to the bed, flipped me over so that I was on all fours and facing away from him, I couldn't help but moan at the feeling of his hands on my ass. He spread me open, as though admiring me, and then leaned forward to plant a warm, wet, sloppy kiss against my slit. I gasped.

"Couldn't let him have all the fun now, could I?" He murmured, and he landed a playful spank on my ass before I heard him unzip his pants and reach for a condom.

Before me, on the other side of the bed, Johnathan was standing, gazing down at me like I was the most beautiful thing in the entire world. I reached out to rub my hand over the bulge in his pants, and he cocked an eyebrow at me.

"You want me, too?" He asked, and I nodded. I didn't even need to speak. I felt as though the three of us were on some other level far removed from conversation right now. We just understood what we all wanted, and we were going to do anything that we could to make sure that we gave it to one another.

He unzipped, slowly, almost like he was doing a striptease, and pulled his cock from his pants. Behind me, I could feel Tommy lining himself up against my pussy for the first time, just as John guided his thick tip to my lips.

I opened my mouth, extended my tongue, and swirled it around him, trying to recall everything I had done to pleasure Ian back in my bathroom. I wanted to make sure that I kept up with them. I knew that I could have just given in to the feeling of being nothing more than a pair of holes for the two of them to fuck, but that would have rather defeated the point of coming here in the first place, wouldn't it? If I was going to do this, then I was going to do this properly, and I was going to make sure that I was a conquest that they'd never forget.

As though on a practiced pace, they both pushed into me for the first time – and God, the feeling of them taking me like that was everything that I needed right now. The fullness was almost a shock; I had never struggled with taking big dicks before, but having two of them at once was something else entirely, and I loved it. For a moment, my body sagged, unable to process the pleasure that they were both giving me and keeping up my part in this – but then, I arched my back, and pushed my hips down against Tommy to take as much of him as I possibly could. I was going to do this *right.* I was sure of it.

"Fuck," Johnathan groaned, and I flicked my eyes up to meet his as I took his cock into my mouth. There was a furrow in his brow, proof that I was doing everything he needed me to right now, and I wanted to make sure that I gave him everything that I could.

Behind me, Tommy had started to pick up the pace, driving himself into me hard and fast. The roughness of it was contradicted and contrasted with the sensuality of the way that Johnathan was letting me blow him. The mix of the two men, of the two styles that they took when it came to taking me, was everything that I needed right now. I was being pushed forward every time Tommy moved into me, taking Johnathan a little deeper every time that I did, as though the two of them were using me as some toy to pleasure each other, a translator to turn each other on.

I thought it would have bugged me, being treated like that. But honestly, the way that they were using me right now, it was like I was a tool meant to give nothing but pleasure, and I was crazy about the way that it made me feel. The power, the passion, the intensity of the way they were taking me was everything that I needed right now. I wanted more. Wanted more than I could take. I wanted to be filled right up to the brim and then pushed a little further beyond that – I wanted it to rush through me, the fullness that they were pushing through me right now.

Tommy's hands came to my hips and he pulled me back, hard, thrusting deep into me, right up to the hilt, so that I could feel his heavy balls slapping up against my pussy with each and every thrust. And God, I was already close – the mixture of having Johnathan go down on me and then to be filled by this delicious, fat cock was everything that I needed right now.

Johnathan's hand came to the back of my head, and I gazed up at him as he began to push himself deeper into my mouth. The feeling of it shocked me, the way that he slipped into me so deliciously I could hardly make sense of it. I found my throat opening, ready to take him, ready to take everything that he had for me.

"You're so good at that," he murmured, and he smoothed my hair back, nearly tenderly, if it hadn't been for the fact that his cock was thrust all the way down my throat. I moaned around his cock, and watched as the vibrations moved up through his body, consuming him. I knew that it wasn't going to be long until he came.

I knew it wasn't going to be long until I did, either. I wanted nothing more than to finish, feel that rough clench of my pussy around his cock as the relief coursed through my body, and I wasn't sure how much more I was going to be able to take. As Tommy filled me from behind, as Johnathan screwed me from the front, I could feel that warm, welcoming rush of pleasure starting to grow inside of me. As though something was boiling inside of me, something fiery with want, need, and desire.

Tommy reached his hand between my legs and began to roughly massage my clit as he fucked me, as though sensing how close I was to the edge at that moment. With my mouth full of Johnathan's cock, it wasn't like I could make much noise to react, but he must have been able to tell from the clenching between my thighs how good it was.

"You nearly there?" He asked me. His voice was playful, almost mocking, as though he was teasing me for being so unable to hold back, and it only sent another surge of want through my system. How could it not?

He shoved himself deep into me one last time and held himself there, letting my pussy massage the contours of his cock – and it was like that, filled with dick from two ends, that I finally felt myself reach my release.

The pleasure consumed me, burning through me like a flame down my spine – Johnathan pulled back for a moment, letting me catch my breath, and I couldn't help but let out this desperate, hungry whine as the orgasm tore through me. As he felt my pussy clenching around his cock, it seemed to give him everything that he needed to reach his own release, and just a few seconds later, I finally felt him finish inside of me.

And it seemed to be the sight of his friend – his lover – finishing in my pussy that took Johnathan over the edge, too. I opened my mouth, told him that I wanted him back, and he pushed himself inside of me just in time for me to feel him finish down my throat. I was becoming quite the expert at making men come with my tongue, wasn't I? I swallowed it down without a second thought, enjoying the sweet sensation of knowing that I had been enough to take them both over the edge.

And, as they drew back from me, I felt my knees buckle as I dived forward on to the bed. I didn't know what I had expected from this night – what I had hoped for, maybe, yes, but not what I actually thought was going to happen. But this? This was everything that I had needed it to be. And I knew that I was far from done with these two for the night. Far from done, yet.

Chapter 6

F/F, Bi-Curious, Fingering

Kaylee sat down and sunk in the couch and looked around my apartment once more; she seemed shocked that I was here at all, let alone that I had managed the first full month of my time alone so well.

"I just can't believe that you really got out from his shit," she remarked, as she took a sip of the wine that I had given her when she had arrived. I grinned at her, lifted my glass in her direction as I sank down onto the seat beside her.

"Trust me, I can't either," I agreed.

"How has it been?" She asked me. After the party, she had been clamoring to get me to herself for a while, and I knew that I had so much to catch her up on it was unreal. It was going to be a lot of fun, I knew that she would hardly be able to wrap her head around the fact that I had come as far as I had – sometimes, it seemed impossible even to me, that I could have unleashed this sex-kittenish version of myself after keeping her locked up for so long.

"It's been kind of crazy," I confessed, and she laughed and sipped on the red that I had brought for us to share tonight.

"Yeah, trust me, I was at that party," she reminds me. "I think I know how crazy you've gotten..."

"Was it really that obvious?" I asked, pulling a face and pretending for a moment like I was totally embarrassed by the fact that everyone knew what I had been getting into. But, when she tipped her head to the side and raised an eyebrow, I dropped it.

"He walked out of there looking like he'd just met God," she reminded me. "I think everyone knew what was going on."

"Wish I could say I regretted it," I fired back cockily, and she busted out laughing.

"Where did this come from?" She asked me, waving her hand in my general direction, gazing at me as though she couldn't believe what she was hearing. "I feel like this is a whole new side of you..."

"So do I," I agreed enthusiastically. "It's just...I feel like I've been trying to keep myself under wraps for so long now, and I don't have any time left to do that. I've got to be honest. I know what I want, and it's..."

"To suck dick?" She filled in for me bluntly.

"Something like that," I replied, flashing her a mysterious smile. For so long, I had just been everyone's good little friend, the girl who would never have gotten into anything that she shouldn't have. And now? Now, I had unleashed some new part of me, and I wanted nothing more than to make sure that everyone understood just what a bad bitch she was.

"Is it really just because you're single now?" She asked with interest. "I mean, I know that you were with him for so long, but I thought you guys had a... good sex life?"

"I thought so too," I replied. "Or at least, I managed to convince myself that we did. But I wanted more than he could ever give me. Really, I know that I deserve it. It's just...I've always wanted more than someone like him could give me, you know?"

"Like what?" She asked, shifting forward with interest. She might have been a wild child back in the day herself but that didn't mean that she wasn't curious to find out just what else might be out there – just what else she might have missed out on.

"Uh, where do you want me to start?" I asked, spreading my hands wide. She cocked her head at me.

"How much is there to hear?"

"A lot," I warned her.

"Then start at the beginning," she replied. My eyes flicked over to the bedroom door, where the moving guy had fucked me right on the day that I had moved in. I knew that she would never have believed me if I had told her, but hey, if she wanted to hear it, right...?

And so, I told her. I told her everything that I had been getting up to since I had come out here. And honestly, even hearing the words come out of my own mouth like that was something of a shock – I couldn't believe that I could say all of this and really mean it, it felt as though it had to be coming from someone else entirely. I knew that I had really been through all of that, but recounting it out loud like this – yeah, that was something new.

By the time that I was done, she had finished her glass of wine, and she was staring at me as though she had never met me before in my life.

"You really...all of it?" She asked. I nodded.

"I really... all of it," I replied, with a chuckle, enjoying how shocked she looked right now. I knew that I was the last person that she would ever have expected to come out with this sort of thing, and if there was one thing that I had found I truly loved about this new life, it was flaunting the expectations that people placed on me.

"I didn't...I guess I just didn't know that you had any of it in you," she remarked, and she lifted the empty glass to her lips again, like she had forgotten that she'd already drained it. I reached over and took it from her, and went to fill it up in the kitchen again.

I could feel her watching me, even as I got her another glass; there was something about the air in the room that felt thicker than normal. I knew that there was something on her mind, something that she wanted to say to me, but that she was too nervous to come out with it.

Which wasn't like her. If there was one thing that I knew about her, it was that she spoke her mind. As I came back to the couch, gave her the glass, I cocked an eyebrow at her.

"Something on your mind?"

"Yeah, honestly," she admitted, and she hesitated before she spoke again. "You...you were with a girl?"

"Yeah, I was," I replied. I still couldn't quite believe that I got to say that and mean it, but I did. It was an odd sensation, being the most experienced person in the room, even if the vast majority of those experiences had come in the last month.

"I've never done that before," she confessed. "But I was always...I mean, I was always curious to know how it would be..."

"Really?" I replied, tipping my head to the side with interest. She nodded.

"Yeah, it just always seemed like something...something I should try," she continued. Her voice seemed to have lifted into a slightly higher plane, as though she was trying to sound casual despite the seriousness of this inside her head.

"You know that you can if you want, right?" I pointed out to her. "I mean, there's nothing stopping you."

"Oh, I wouldn't know where to start," she admitted, a small pink flush tinging in her cheeks. "It would just be — no. I don't think it would be something I could do without seeming like the straightest straight girl ever, you know?"

"I guess," I replied. "But everyone has to start somewhere, don't they?"

"Sure, but where...where do I even begin with that?" She replied, as her eyes met mine again. And suddenly, it hit me what was going on here. She was hinting. Hinting to me that she wanted me to be the one to show her how all of this was done.

I would have been lying if I said I wasn't a little flattered to realize that she wanted that from me. Had I become, all at once, this arbiter of all things gay? I wouldn't have minded one little bit. At least, in this circumstance.

"Are you asking me to show you?" I murmured to her. I watched her breath catch, her entire body start for an instant, and I couldn't help but smile. I wanted this. I wanted to find out what was going to happen if I just shifted an inch towards her, just moved closer and closer. She didn't pull away from me. Her eyes were still stuck on mine, her lips slightly parted, as though there was something that she wanted to say to me but that she had no idea how to say it.

I knew how she felt, and I wanted to make sure that I gave her everything that I could to prove that this was real. My mind flooded back to the first time that I had been looked at in that way, by another woman, a woman who had seemed to want me, really desire me. The way it had flicked a switch inside my head, turned me into something else.

I reached out, traced a finger down her cheek. She closed her eyes. There was no going back no – no denying the fact that this was real, that this was happening, that we were doing this. I brushed my finger over her lips, and watched the way her tongue curled out to taste my skin, as though she was starving for me.

And I couldn't help but push my fingers forward, into the warmth of her mouth. She closed her eyes for a moment, and I leaned closer, marveling at the way that she reacted to me – enjoying the look of surprise on her face, the way she seemed to start when I was close to her. I skimmed my fingers down her waist, and found my hand on her pants, undoing them, pulling them away from her body. She arched her hips from the couch as she slid her tongue against my fingerprints, tasting me.

I drew my fingers from her mouth, and moved them down, leaving a line of her own saliva on her skin as I inched further and further down her body – marking a line down between her breasts, watching the way that her chest rose and fell like she was crying out for me to do more, to give her more. And I wanted to – God, I wanted to. I could already feel the pressure building between my own legs, the weight of it starting to draw my attention in a way that I couldn't deny.

As soon as my hand reached between her legs, I kissed her – properly this time, not the chaste peck that I had planted on her cheek when she had come through the door, all smiles and giggles and pretending we were nothing more than friends. I wondered if there had been some part of her that had been longing for this from the start. Maybe she had seen some other side of me at the party, and that it had drawn out a fascination in her that she had been nurturing ever since. Honestly, the mere idea of that was enough to send shivers of excitement through my system. I was obsessed with her, with the idea that she might have wanted me all along.

I brushed my fingers over her bush as I pushed my fingers into her panties, feeling her breath catch in the back of her throat for a split second in the moment before I found her clit. She moaned against my lips as soon as I did, and I felt that thrill of control, of power, of dominance. I was the one who knew what they were doing here, I was the one who made the rules and showed her just how to run things. It had been a while since I had felt like I had actually got some claim over any of this, since I had felt as though I was the one in charge.

Her tongue spoke against mine, as though all the words that we had said up until this point to one another had been nothing close to enough. I knew how she felt. The pressure of her body against mine had taken this somewhere else, somewhere new, somewhere that I had never even realized that it needed to be – when she touched me, pushed her hand through my hair, I knew that we had taken this to a level that we were never going to be able to bring it back from.

And I didn't mind one tiny little bit.

No, I wanted to find out where we could go next. As I massaged her clit with two fingers, our lips moving softly against one another's, I knew that I wasn't going to be satisfied until I'd made her come. I had never made another woman come before, not just with my touch, and I had to find out what it was like.

I slipped my fingers down a little further, to the wetness of her slit, and pulled that slickness back to her clit for lubrication; she lifted her hips and started to push back against me, letting me use her the way I wanted to. I knew that this was already spinning out of control. I knew that this was already going further than we had ever been ready for it to. And now – and now, there was nothing that I could do but give in to the way it felt to have her pushing back against me like this. Grinding on my hand like I was the only thing in the entire world that she wanted right now.

"Fuck," she gasped against my lips, and I kissed her again, harder this time, exploring her lips and her mouth with my own. In all the time that I had known her, I had never looked at her and craved something like this – but now that she was here, giving herself to me like this, handing her pleasure to me on a platter, I knew that there was no way that I could turn her down. The thrill of being in charge here, that was all that I had needed, and, as I kissed her deeply and played with her clit, I knew that I could have done this the whole night through if she had asked it of me.

I had no idea what I was expecting when she came – but it didn't take long till I felt the shockwaves of her body tensing, her entire system shaking against mine for a moment. I could taste the wine on her lips as I stilled my fingers against her clit, feeling her pussy spasming against my hand, and wondering if that was what I had been waiting for.

But, as she slumped back on to the couch to catch her breath, I couldn't help but grin. I knew that I had done it. I had taken her there. I watched as she stared at the ceiling, her chest rising and falling fast, her jaw trembling as though the shockwaves of all of this were pulsing through her still. I drew my fingers to my mouth, tasting her wetness upon them, and wondering why it was that the mere scent of her turned me on so much.

"How was it?" I asked her, as I rose to my feet, and went to grab myself another glass of wine again. She lifted her head so that she could look up at me, her gaze so distant and so lost to happiness that she seemed unable to control herself.

"It was..." she breathed, and I knew that she wasn't going to be able to come up with anything more impressive than that. I didn't care. I had just successfully made a woman come all by myself for the first time, and I was pretty damn proud of myself for pulling it off. Maybe I was starting to come out the other side of my sexual education – maybe I was starting to turn into the very person that I had always longed to be, the one in total and utter control of her sexuality and everything around it.

As I poured myself another glass and took a sip, mixing her sweet muskiness with the scent of the wine in my mouth, I grinned to myself. There was still so much for me to learn, and I wanted to find out exactly what this

world still had to show me. Because I was sure that I
would pass with flying colors.

Chapter 7

F/F, Masturbation, Sex Toys

I pushed my door open, flopped down on the couch, and let out a long sigh. Ugh. It had already been one hell of a long week. And I felt like I was starting to lose my grip on the woman that I had been longing to become.

I had been at work every single shift from start to finish ever since one of our other baristas had quit. And normally, I wouldn't have minded putting in the time for them – after all, I had worked there for years, and it wasn't like my boss hadn't overlooked a few hungover shifts and the like – but that was the old me. That was the version of me that didn't have as much to claim to her name as she did now, and I didn't want to let that slip through my fingers.

It had been a week since I had seen Kaylee, since we'd fooled around on my couch, and normally, a week since my last sexual encounter would have been more than enough to keep me satisfied. But that had been then, this was now, and I was used to getting pretty much anything that I wanted as soon as I got the inkling that I'd have liked it. I was getting greedy. And I knew that I was going to have to take things to the next level if I was going to make sure that I kept things going the way that they needed to be.

I'd seen Tommy at work, a few days ago; I swear, it was just the sight of him that had sent me so crazy up in my own head, the memory of everything that I had gotten up to when I had been with him and Johnathan not that long ago. It had been a hell of a lot of fun, and I could tell from the way he flirted with me over the coffee that I made for him, that he wanted to do it all over again. And trust me, I would have been lying if I'd said that I wasn't a little curious to find out what else I could get into with the two of them – but I needed something new right now. Something I had never experienced before.

I knew that I wasn't going to have time to do much else but go home and get as much sleep as I could this weekend, and so, I had ordered myself something to take the edge off of my need – a collection of sex toys, paid-for by my last paycheck. I knew that I probably should have saved it for sensible things like takeout and wine, but honestly, I wanted to have a collection that I knew I could delve into whenever I needed to. I wanted to be able to rely on myself, no matter what – wanted to be sure that I always had something fun to come back to right here at home if I craved it.

And that's what I stayed focused on, over anything else. I got through all of my shifts that week sneakily checking on the shipping details for the toys that were headed in my direction, hoping that they would be there by the time I rounded off my run of shifts at the start of the weekend. I intended to lock that door, and indulge myself in all the ways that I could think of. It was self-care, wasn't it? Something like that...

And, sure enough, I spotted the package sitting next to my door when I went out to check on my mail. Yes! I grabbed it, shook it a couple of times to make sure that it was heavy enough to contain everything that I needed it to, and then dived back into my apartment to do what I needed to do.

I was going to make this an *event.* If I was going to do this, I was going to do it properly, and that meant starting slow, taking my time and really indulging myself in everything that I wanted to engage with. I ran myself a bath, dripped in a few drops of the expensive bath oil that someone had left for me after I had invited them round for the housewarming party, and sank beneath the water, closing my eyes and letting it soothe my sore muscles and tired spirit.

With the box next to the bath, I reached over without opening my eyes to pull out something new. My fingers closed around a long, slender dildo; I had picked out a few dildos of different sizes and shapes, wanting to find out what worked best for me, mainly so that I would be able to tell at a glance whose cock would feel the best before I fucked them. I figured that I was going to have to streamline all my sexual exploits if I was going to get the most out of them, and this seemed like an appropriate way to do it.

I pushed the toy beneath the water, admiring the slender contours of its pink, silicone length; it wasn't meant to look anything like an actual dick, I assumed, but that didn't matter. It was longer than anything I had actually had inside of me, and I wasn't sure that I would be able to take every inch of it, but hey – a girl could only try, couldn't she?

I took my time with it, sliding it over my clit a couple of times to get myself used to the slick feel of the toy against my skin – it was so new, so fresh, that I found my pussy responding to it almost at once, needing to find the relief that only something deep inside of me could give me.

Eventually, I let it slide down to my pussy, teasing it around the edges of my slit for a moment. I bit my lip, smiled. See? Who needed a man, when I had something like this to give me everything that I needed right now? Finally, I started to guide it inside of me, taking my time, sliding it slow and deep into my pussy, and feeling my slit spread to take every inch of it.

I watched, almost amazed, as it vanished inside of me. I knew that I had taken a lot down there in the last few weeks – a lot everywhere else, too, if I was being honest – but that didn't mean that I still didn't find myself wondering if I could really take it as far as this. My body tensed as I felt it plunge deeper into me, filling me, so deep that I was sure it wouldn't be long until it was lost inside me forever.

"Mmmm," I groaned theatrically. I knew that I didn't need to perform for anyone, but damn, there was something fun in making the noises, playing the game a little. I was sure that anyone who overheard me would have thought that I was crazy for playing it up like this, but as I tipped my head back, let my body slide down a little further under the steaming water, I groaned again. The fullness was delicious, enough to let the tension begin to leak from me, and soon, I found myself sliding it in and out of me deeper, harder, enjoying the grinding pressure that it sent between my legs, up throughout my entire body.

"Fuck," I gasped to myself. There was something freeing about knowing that I didn't have to worry about looking or sounding good, moving in a certain way that would prove that I was worth everything that the other person was giving me. I screwed up my face in pleasure, moved my other hand down so that I could play with my clit as I fucked myself. The oil in the water was clinging to my skin in the most delicious way imaginable, the touch of it so delicious that I could feel it prickling from the top of my scalp down to the tips of my toes.

I spread my legs further, hooked one ankle over the side of the bathtub, and pushed that toy in even deeper, harder. I didn't have to ask anyone to give it to me, I could just gift myself this delicious feeling, the treat of being fucked just the way that I wanted to be fucked.

And it didn't take long till all the tension that had been building between my thighs, deep in my belly, all week long started to consume me. I tipped my head back, almost submerged beneath the steaming hot water, and finally, finally, felt the orgasm shudder through my entire body at once.

I made a noise unlike anything I had heard come out of myself before. Because I wasn't moderating it to make sure that it didn't put anyone off – I was just doing what came naturally to me, letting the pleasure take control of me and choosing how I reacted in that moment. I felt my pussy clench around the toy, and I held it there, deep inside of me, my hand stilled over my clit, my whole body frozen in that moment of pleasure that made everything fade to black at the edges.

As I came back into my body again, it took me a moment to remember that I was actually still in the bath – the orgasm had been so intense that I couldn't think straight, and the feelings that were still pulsing through me made my head spin.

I pulled the toy from between my legs and dropped it over the edge of the tub, back into the box once more. Fuck, yes. That was all that I had needed. And even now, I didn't have to worry about getting anyone else off, have to worry about making sure I kept performing for somebody else who might have been watching or fucking me. This was just all about me, the indulgence that I could give to myself once and for all.

I lay back, let my hair float out around me in what must have looked like a halo to anyone else watching. Not that there was anyone else to watch right now. No, because this was all about me. Me, and me alone. And I wanted to make the very most of that time that I had to myself while I still could. Was there something to be said for someone else to keep you company – maybe even more than one person? Sure. But right now, I was all about indulging my own whims. And that was the way I was planning to keep it.

Chapter 8

F, Solo, Performance, Exhibitionist

I started up the laptop, bit my lip, and stared at the screen as I waited for it to come to life in front of me. I couldn't believe I was actually doing this. I couldn't believe I was actually going to see this through.

It had crossed my mind the night before, when I had been using that new little bullet vibrator that I had purchased to get myself off before I went to sleep. How much fun it would be to show this side of myself to someone else. Of course, I didn't want to do it in person – no, this weekend, I had decided, was about nothing more than the thrill of giving myself over to pleasure, the pleasure that I could deliver to myself, and nothing more than that.

But there were plenty of people out there who would have taken me exactly as I was. And I was determined to find out just how far they might have gone to show me just how much they enjoyed me.

I had woken up early that morning, and had found my mind already racing with a million questions, a million wonderings as to how I could make that happen. It didn't take long for me to track down forums where like-minded adults with the same penchant for sexuality seemed willing to share everything they've got up to, and I signed up at once and logged myself in. And, when I saw for myself what they've been getting into – I could hardly believe it.

Okay, so I knew that I had been pretty wild by any measurement system when it came to real life. But this? This was something else entirely, and I didn't know how to wrap my head around it. They were posting pictures, videos, stories, everything that they could, and seemingly focusing on their own exploits to fill out the details. I watched with fascination as a woman, her head just out of frame so that her identity was disguised, masturbated herself to orgasm, groaning loudly as she flopped back on the bed. The camera had managed to capture the pulsations of her pussy, and the sight of it was already starting to turn me on.

Not just because I wanted to be there with her, though that was a part of it. But because of the stream of texts up the side of her video – live-chat, people responding to her performance, telling her how sexy she was to them, how much they wished that they could be there with her, all of the things that they would have done to her if they had gotten even half of a chance to do so. I couldn't take my eyes off of that part, the things that they were telling her, and I knew at once that I had to find out what else I could do to get this kind of response.

I had never been the most tech-savvy person in the world, but I could get my laptop camera set up to shoot me – and make sure that I didn't show off my face in the process. I knew that the café I worked for was pretty liberal, but that didn't mean that I wanted images of myself mid-orgasm open-sourced for anyone who wanted them. I wasn't looking to become a porn star – well, not yet, anyway – and I just wanted to capture the attention of the perverts on this site along with me.

Once I had logged myself in, I spent a little while fussing over the set-up of the camera, making sure that it was exactly how I wanted it to be. I had positioned it next to the bed, playing it almost as a candid shot that I had been caught in the middle of. I wanted this to feel natural, even though I was going to be putting on the performance of a lifetime for whoever happened to be tuned in to the forum at that moment.

I climbed on to the bed, and looked at myself, reflected in the screen in front of me. I had to admit, I liked the way that my body looked right now – for a long time, I had been so busy beating myself up about the smallest details of the way that I looked that I had failed to notice that the whole picture really wasn't all that bad. I liked the way my body was, liked the way it moved. I swayed back and forth a little, admiring the curve of my hips, the way my waist slid in before it made space for my breasts. I ran my hand over my nipples, pinching them so that they were swollen and pink and clearly visible in the camera. I bit my lip, smiled. Okay, I didn't even need to turn that thing on right now, it seemed. I was more than willing to just get off on the way that I looked right now...

But I wanted to find out what would have happened if I took things to the next level. Just the next one. To find out what they would think of me. One of the things that

I liked the most about this place was that they always seemed to find something sweet to say about the girls or the guys who put themselves out there. Nobody was treated like they were less-than, nobody was treated as though they weren't good enough. And God, I needed to know that much – I might have been embracing parts of myself I never would have before, but that didn't mean that my ego would have been able to take it if I had received some horrible feedback from someone who had been watching my feed.

I hovered my finger over the button that would allow me to broadcast live. This was my last chance to back out. As soon as I hit that thing, I wasn't going to be able to deny it any longer – I was going to have to deal with whatever those people thought of me, whether it turned out to be good or bad.

And I couldn't wait to find out what they were going to say.

I pressed the button, moved back on the bed, and made sure that I had the collection of toys in arm's reach. I was totally naked, save for a pair of panties, and I knew that whoever was going to log in and spot me was going to be in for a surprise.

I counted down the seconds – one, two, three – before someone popped in to watch my feed. My heart flipped in my chest, and I made double-sure that nobody could see my face.

"Hey," I greeted them. I didn't know whether they were a man, woman, something else entirely, but I didn't care.

I just wanted to perform. I just wanted to show myself off to them and prove that I could give them anything and everything that they might have wanted. A message popped up into the chat, which I had enlarged to make sure that I could see it without moving from the bed.

You're gorgeous.

"Thank you," I giggled happily, and I twisted my body this way and that way a little, showing myself off for the enjoyment of whoever might have been seeing me in that moment. I wanted nothing more than to be admired, to be wanted, to be longed-for. Even if they couldn't touch me, they could still show me what they wanted, right?

"Can I show you something?" I asked flirtatiously. Another person who popped into the chat, told me *yes, yes, yes.* I reached into the box beside me and withdrew a small vibrator, spreading my legs and pushing myself up on my knees so that they would be able to see me properly. My heart was pounding, my adrenalin was pumping, and I couldn't believe that this was actually happening right now. Couldn't believe that I would actually be willing to go through with something so filthy.

But here I was. And there was no way that I was going to back out now.

I clicked the vibrator on in my hand, and pushed it down between my legs, underneath the panties that I was wearing. My lips parted theatrically as I felt it press against my clit, even though nobody else could see it. I gasped loudly, arching my back to push myself against the toy a little harder. A flurry of message notifications pinged up at once, and I took a long moment to toy with myself before I opened my eyes to see who they might have been from.

My eyes widened when I realized just how many people were watching my stream right now. At least twenty different users had sent me messages. And that wasn't even counting the ones who hadn't had a chance to yet – who were maybe too distracted by the show that I was putting on to think about it. I felt a surge of lust dance through my body as I realized just how much they wanted me, just how much they desired me. I couldn't remember the last time that I had felt this dizzy with desire, and I was glad that I had the vibrator pressed against my clit right now, because otherwise, I might not have been able to control myself.

"Fuck," I groaned, and I began to move my hand with more purpose beneath my panties, making sure that the people on the other end of this show could see how wet my underwear had already become just at the knowledge that they were watching. I squinted to read the messages as I played with myself. One of them was asking me to turn around and show them my ass, and I shifted on the spot, bent over, arched my back so that they could get a look at me.

"You like?" I flirted with them. I knew that I was risking showing my face right now, but I didn't care. All that I could focus on was the thrill of desire coursing through me right now, the power that I felt like I had over all of these men. My pussy was burning with want as I felt a million digital eyes on me, watching me, taking me in and admiring me at once.

I started to thrust my hips back against the vibrator – being on all fours like this, so exposed, was just the hottest thing to me. I couldn't resist reaching around behind myself to pull my panties aside, to show myself off to the people who were watching me. I wanted them to see all of me. I wanted them to take in every inch of my body, and the thrill of knowing that I didn't even have a clue who they were only made it more intense.

I heard the messages again, and I couldn't resist moving so that I could read them, making an effort to keep myself out of the frame; a dozen of them were asking me to show my face, so at least I knew that I hadn't managed to screw that one up. But the others were telling me how gorgeous I was, how sexy, asking me to bend this way and that way, asking me to show myself off and touch myself and get naked and – well, more than I would ever be able to do in just one of these little streams.

And besides, this was about me. I was gifting them with my presence, and I wasn't going to let anyone tell me how to do this. I planted one hand behind me, leaned back into it, and rolled the vibrator against my clit in circles. I was going to come soon, I could feel it, going to come harder than I had come in a long time. Maybe it was just the intensity of all the people watching me, knowing that there were so many out there getting off to the sight of me doing the same thing.

I thrust my hips against the vibrator, over and over again, losing myself to the way that it felt, to the feeling of the vibrations pulsing up and through my body. I felt as though every nerve-ending was alight with desire, and knowing that I was likely cresting towards the climax at the same time as the other people watching me just made it even better.

When I came, I didn't make a sound. I knew that they would all be able to tell from just looking at me what had happened. My whole body spasmed with pleasure, and I nearly crumpled into the bed in relief, only remembering at the very last second that I was making sure that they couldn't see my face. I pulled the vibrator out and tossed it aside, breathing hard, my tits shaking as I tried to come back down to Earth once more…

And it was only then, after I was sure that I was done, that I reached over and turned off the video. And finally let myself down in front of the laptop so that I could see what they had all been saying about me.

The thrill of seeing everything that they had said about me, my body, my pleasure, the way I moved, was almost enough to start a burning desire rising in me again. But I was so exhausted from the adrenalin that I could only lean against the bed and catch my breath. Enjoying the compliments still pouring in to me, the questions as to when I was going to be around to do that again.

But there was one message that stood out to me – one message that made me slow and stop in my tracks, a message that made me smile at once. A message that I knew there was no way in hell that I was going to be able to ignore.

A message from a man telling me that he wanted to meet me in person. And a specific list of all the things that he would do to me when he got the chance.

Chapter 9

M/F, Strangers, Soft Male Dom

I sat there, in the hotel bar, and stared down at the drink that I had poured for myself. I wanted nothing more than to down it to try and take the edge off everything that was going through my brain right now, but I knew that I wanted to be totally sober for when Tobe turned up.

I still couldn't believe I was doing this. Couldn't believe that I was actually thinking about hooking up with a man that I had never met before in my life. Of everything that I had done so far, on my long mission to uncover all the deepest desires in my sexuality, this was the craziest.

And maybe that's why it was the one I had been most excited about from the start.

Tobe and I had been talking for two weeks, on and off, ever since he had spotted the little live performance that I'd shared on that forum. I wasn't sure what it was about his message that had drawn me in – maybe just the fact that he had good grammar, compared to the rest of the people who had been horny-contacting me ever since – but I was fascinated by him at once. I had to find out if he could follow through on everything that he had said that he would do for me, and he was passing through my city at the end of the week on a work trip from somewhere else entirely. If I was going to find out if he could put his money where his mouth was, then it was going to be now, or never.

He had given me the name of the hotel that he was staying at, and we had agreed to share a couple of drinks at the bar before we did anything else. Much as I was tempted to just dive into everything that he could give me – to find out just how far he was really willing to take this – I knew that it was better for my own safety to play it cool. I had made sure to tell Kaylee where I was right now, even though she tried to convince me not to go at all. Honestly, I wouldn't have been surprised if she was a little jealous. She had been acting more than a little possessive of me since the night that we had fooled around together, and I was sure that she wanted a little more to come of what we had done there considering everything that I had given her.

Anyway, tonight, I wasn't about women. I was about men. Well, one man. One man who had promised that he would give me the fucking of my life. And I wanted to find out if he could follow through on it.

I had arrived a little earlier than we had agreed upon. I wanted to make sure that I had a feel for the place before he got there; he was coming from some big work meeting, he had told me, though I couldn't for the life of me remember what he actually did for a living. I still couldn't believe that I was even considering going with someone I didn't know at all; I knew that I had hooked up with Johnathan without really knowing much about him, but that was different. He came with a stamp of approval from someone that I actually knew, someone that I actually trusted. But Tobe? Tobe could have been anyone. And that was what I was most excited about.

I supposed it was the same as the way the anonymity of the people who had watched me thrilled me down to my core; I liked the thought of this, the thought of giving myself over to someone who knew nothing about me. They wouldn't come with any expectations, they would just take me as I was. And I wanted to know how that would play out.

And so, when I finally locked eyes with him walking into the bar, my heart skipped several beats. He had sent me a few pictures of himself, and truly, I had been ready for them to be a little more flattering than he actually turned out to be in real life. But, if anything, he was even cuter in person; dark hair, flecked with distinguished gray, blue eyes, a little light stubble that seemed intentional. Fancy suit, expensive tie. He greeted me with a kiss on the cheek, swooping down to plant a peck against my skin and nearly making me swoon in the process.

"It's lovely to finally meet you," He told me, and I could tell from the way his eyes seemed to melt into mine that he meant it. I nodded. I knew that I was meant to say something back in response, but I didn't know quite how to do it. I was just so dazzled by the fact that this guy was actually hot.

He sank down into the seat opposite me, not taking his eyes off of me for a moment. I stared back at him. I wanted to say something, but I wasn't sure what. We had been talking pure filth to each other, all the time that we had been chatting online, and I would have been lying if I'd said that it wasn't the only thing on my mind right about now. I wished that I could just reach into my head and pull out all the stuff that was rushing through it, all the things that I wanted to do to him.

He waved down a waiter and ordered a drink, and finally, I went about digging up what remained of my voice once more.

"I can't believe I'm really doing this," I confessed. He cocked his head to the side with interest.

"Why so?"

"I've never...I mean, I've never just met up with someone like this for..." I trailed off. I didn't know how to fill in the rest of that sentence. Even though I had sent him things that were far worse than anything running through my head in that moment, I wasn't sure that I would be able to say them out loud.

"Trust me, it's a lot more fun than it's given credit for," he replied, and he moved his hand to mine with confidence – his touch sent a shiver down my spine, the way he looked at me impossible to deny.

"You don't have to worry about what they might think of you, because chances are, you're never going to see them again," he explained. "You just have to worry about your pleasure. Asking for everything that you've always been too afraid to. Though I doubt there's much that you haven't asked for over the years..."

His eyes scanned down my body, to the generous hit of cleavage that I was showing off over the top of my dress, and I felt a flush hit my cheeks. Fuck, I wanted this man. He was right. There was an undeniable thrill to the thought of just – of just knowing that I could take anything that I wanted from him, and he would be gone by the time that dawn broke the next day. I crossed my legs, squeezed my thighs together, and hoped to God that he wouldn't be able to tell how unremittingly horny I was right now. I didn't want him to think that I was too easy or something...

But then, what was the point of pretending? If I wanted pleasure, then I was going to take it, and this man seemed more than willing to give it to me any single way that he could. I loved that. And I wanted to prove to him that I could keep up with him any way he wanted me to.

I leaned towards him, making sure that I pressed my tits together as I did so – I watched his eyes lower to my breasts, and I knew that he was having a hard time keeping his hands off of them right then and there.

"Let's go to your room," I murmured to him, and I tossed my hair over one shoulder, hoping that if I played the seductress, I would start to feel it, too.

I rose to my feet, and a moment later, he did the same to follow me. I didn't know where I was going, so when I felt his hand slide around my waist, I was relieved that I wasn't going to have to keep up this act any longer. I wanted nothing more than to just have him take me right then and right there, but I knew I had to play it a little more carefully than that.

He walked me up to his room, and to anyone who might have passed us by, we would have looked nothing more than a couple going back to our place after a romantic night on the town. Little did they know that we had never met before, that I didn't even know this man's last name – hell, I didn't even know if the first name that he had given me was accurate, and I was more than willing to make sure that he knew as little about me as I did about him. In fact, by the time I left this place, I wanted to make sure that the only thing that he was sure of about me was the fact that I was the best lay he'd ever had in his life. After all, he had found me, online, making myself come – the least I could do was see through that fantasy for him, wasn't it?

As soon as we reached the door, I grabbed for his shirt, and pulled him close to me. Our lips met, and I kissed him hard, marveling at how new this all was to me – marveling at how easy it had been to share myself with a man like this, without even having kissed him before. I had been texting him all about my deepest, darkest desires, and only now was I feeling his hands on my body for the first time.

He pushed the keycard into the lock without pulling back from me, and the two of us tumbled over the door together – his hands started to roam my body at once, his touch sending shockwaves of pleasure through me as he groped at my ass, my tits, my thighs, my stomach. He seemed to want to make sure that I was actually here, that I was truly real, after he had first encountered me in cyberspace like that. I didn't blame him. I knew that I wanted to be certain that he was really there, after the build-up our relationship had taken so far.

He kissed over my neck, my chin, pushing the straps of my dress down so that he could lower his mouth to my breasts. He was rougher than anyone else I had been with, baring his teeth against my nipples and making me cry out with a delicious mix of pain and pleasure. I couldn't get enough. I cradled his head right there for a moment, before he pushed me down onto the bed and climbed on top of me.

He ripped off my dress as though it was nothing more than a slight distraction between him and I; I knew that I had nothing to worry about in his desire for me. I had been a little concerned that things might not feel as fiery since we had only known each other online before this, but if anything, this was even more intense than I had predicted.

He kissed me again, pulled off my panties, and tossed them aside – his hands, now on my naked body, took control of me.

"You have no idea how long I've been waiting to have you like this," he growled into my ear, as I felt his cock begin to swell against my hip. "Ever since I saw you in that live-stream, I knew that I had to have you..."

The dominance in his voice made me ache for him in a way so intense it was almost painful, and my entire system was crying out for him, for as much as I could get from him. I pushed my hands through his hair and pulled him to my mouth again, remembering what he had said when we had met in the bar. That we could do anything that we wanted. We would never have to see each other again after this, and that meant that we could give in to those dark, crazy desires that we might have tried to hide from someone else.

"Spank my ass," I breathed in his ear. It was a test, really, just to see if he would do it. I didn't know how far he would be willing to take this, but the thought of this older man, taking control of me, showing me how he did things, made my pussy ache more than I could handle.

He flipped me over without a second thought, and smoothed his hand over my ass, like he was preparing a canvas for his masterpiece. And then, all at once, he brought his hand down upon me with a sharp slap that made me jump with surprise.

"Oh!" I squeaked. More at the surprise that it felt as good as it did than anything – I had expected myself to be a baby about the pain, but to my shock, it mellowed into something delicious as soon as he began to rub his hand over the impact site again.

"Good?" He asked. I could hear a near-smugness in his voice as he spoke to me, and I knew that he was enjoying making sure that I got off on the feeling of his hands on me. I nodded, glanced over my shoulder, to see him leaning down to plant a kiss on my ass. I remembered the first time that I had put on a little show back on that site, when I had pulled my panties aside to show everyone my pussy and my ass. Seemed like that had made a real impression on him, huh?

"Good," I replied, and he landed another slap on my other ass-cheek – I cried out, but this time, it was in nothing but total and utter pleasure. I was stunned at how good it felt, how good it was to submit to him like this – how easy I found it to let those feelings course through me. I closed my eyes, rested my head on the pillow, I almost felt as though I was getting a massage or something. But instead of rubbing out the knots in my muscles, he was spanking them out, instead. And I had every intention of making sure I enjoyed it as much as I would have if it had been a therapeutic massage.

He was gentle with me – I had seen videos where people went seriously hardcore with the spankings that they received, but he was careful, keeping it light and playful, while making sure that I knew who the one in charge was. It didn't take long till I could feel some wetness leaking down the inside of my thighs, and he noticed it too. Pushing his hand between my legs, he rubbed at my slit roughly, and I groaned. I wished that I had the words to tell him how good that felt, but I didn't.

"You're so wet, baby," he murmured, and he pulled his hand from between my legs and reached around to push it into my mouth. The taste of my muskiness on his fingers was everything that I needed it to be right now, and I sucked hard, rolling his fingers around my mouth, letting my tongue bathe him clean.

"You want me to fuck you?" He asked, pulling his fingers from my mouth and taking his time as he rubbed them over my slit once more – not pushing inside, just moving around me, letting me wait for him. I nodded.

"Say it," he ordered me. I clenched my teeth. There was a naturally defiant part of me that wanted to push back against him, but I knew that it wouldn't have gotten me anywhere. I wanted to feel his dick deep inside my pussy, and I wanted to feel it now.

"Fuck me," I hissed. And that was everything that he wanted to hear from me right now.

I heard the rip of a condom, the zip of his pants, and then, he grabbed my hips and pulled them back towards him. His tip pressed against my entrance and I groaned with an almost painful need. I wanted him to fuck me so hard I couldn't walk the next day. I wanted to feel his cock take me every way that I needed to be taken. I'd been stuck with nothing but the toys for a while now, and honestly, they weren't the same as having a real man, really wanting you, right there and ready to fuck.

He thrust inside of me in one motion, and my whole body trembled, slumping down into the bed so that only my hips were still pointed up to him. His hands were digging into my ass, spreading me wide as he slipped himself all the way inside of me, and I swear, it took everything that I had to keep from reaching around and pulling him into me even deeper.

I loved the way that it felt. Loved the feeling of his thickness inside of me. I couldn't even see his face, but I could feel the grip of his hands, I could feel him pulling me back into him hard, I could hear the sharp breaths that he was letting out right now, and I knew that this was everything that I needed. He wanted me, really wanted me, and knowing that he had wanted me from the moment that he had seen me performing in that stream was only getting me hotter.

He fucked me, thrust into me over and over again, until the only sound in the room was that of our flesh coming together and my helpless little moans of want. I managed to lift my head for a moment, turn to look over my shoulder. There was a darkness to his eyes that thrilled me and aroused me in the same moment – I knew that this was dangerous, but in the best way possible. That kind of measured risk that I always wanted to take, always craved more than I could put into words.

I turned back to grab the headboard and start pushing down against him properly. Fuck, yes – the fullness that coursed through me as he fucked me made my entire head spin, my brain narrowing down to just the thought of how good it felt to be with him, how much I wanted more.

I closed my eyes and tipped my head back, letting out a deep groan of pleasure that reverberated through my whole body, and pushed my hand between my legs to play with myself while he fucked me. I needed this. I needed more. I needed to know that I didn't have to worry about hiding my want or playing demure or anything like that. I just needed to take, take, take everything that I could get, and then, and only then, would I be satisfied.

He pressed his hips against mine and held himself there for a long moment, not pulling back as he kept his cock lodged all the way inside of me, grinding against me and making me squirm. The feeling of that fullness matched with the frantic motion of my fingers between my legs was taking me there, taking me to where I needed to go.

When I felt the orgasm crest, the climax took control of me, I let out a noise that I had never heard come from me in my entire life – the insides of my thighs were trembling with helpless pleasure, and I balled a handful of the covers in my fists to try and expel some of the tension that was riding and rising through my body. He held himself there, merciless, not pulling back, until he seemed satisfied that I had taken what I needed. And then, he began to pound into me again, harder than before, filling me deep, taking me, and then pushing himself over the edge in the moments right after I had done the same.

"Fuck," he growled, as he finished inside of me. I could feel his cock twitching, and I continued to move and grind against him, taking him deeper, taking as much of him as I could manage. I wanted him. I wanted this – I wanted more. I knew that he had just come, but that didn't mean that this had to be over, did it?

I flipped around, reached for him, and pulled him on top of me. I could feel the tension had left his strong body, and that thrilled me. I had reduced this man, boiled him down to his bare essentials, and I loved that. He might have been the one in control when all of this started, but I was the one in charge now, and there wasn't a hope in hell that I was going to let him forget it.

"I'm not done with you yet," I murmured to him, and I felt him grin against my neck as he moved to kiss me again. We had a whole lot left to discover about one another before this night was done. And I wanted to delve into the depths of everything that I'd been trying to hold back all this time.

Chapter 10

M/F, BDSM, Male Dom, Spanking, Binding

I swear, I walked with a swagger after that.

After the night I spent with Tobe – or whatever his name really might have been – in that hotel, it became clear to me that I had something that most people could only dream of. Confidence. Sureness. The certainty that my pussy was good enough to get pretty much any man to do pretty much anything that I wanted him to.

I had slipped out of his room first thing in the morning, before he'd had a chance to wake up. There was just something so naughty and so damn fun about the thought of sneaking away before he'd come to, knowing that the night we'd spent together had been nothing more than what I wanted it to be. He had dropped me a text to make sure that I'd gotten home okay, and I had assured him that I had. Oh, and sent him a picture of a couple of the red hand-marks on my ass from wear he had been spanking me, just for good measure.

I still couldn't believe that I had the nerve to do something like that these days. Back when I had been with my ex, I wouldn't have even dared to snap a picture of myself in my underwear, let alone naked. Let alone send it to someone that I barely knew. Let alone have had *sex* with that person that I barely knew. It was all so fresh to me, so thrilling to realize how much I got out of this kind of lifestyle. I had been sure that I was too uptight for this, but the more time that passed, the more certain I became that I had only scratched the surface of everything that I wanted to enjoy.

Honestly, the best part of my encounter with Tobe had been the power dynamic that we had exchanged – I had allowed him to take control the way he wanted to, and found some delicious relief in knowing that I didn't have to worry about what I was going to do next. I had dabbled in the idea of exchanging power like that, but this was the first time that I had actually gone ahead and done it.

There was more out there for me to explore in that world, I was sure of it. And now that I felt as though I had vanilla sex down – pretty much every version of it that I could imagine – I figured that it was only right I start expanding into what else the world had to offer. Even if I had no clue what that might have looked like.

If there was one person I trusted to help me into this particular side of sex, it was Tommy – and luckily, I still had his number. I dropped him a message, and he agreed to come out for a coffee with me to talk this stuff over. I was glad to have a ticket into the deviance that I knew must have been out there in this city, and truly, even happier that I got to pass the time with a cute guy like Tommy in the process.

"So, what is it exactly you're looking to get into?" He asked me. Now that we had sex off the table – or at least, our first time – I felt like I could actually talk to him like a real person, instead of dealing with the constant level of flirtation that he usually threw at me. I doubted that we would never end up in bed together again – in fact, I was already trying to push to the back of my mind the urge to ask when his friend Johnathan would be back in town once more – but for the time being, I just wanted to pick his brains a little.

"I just want to explore a little bit," I confessed. "I know that there's loads out there, and I'm not entirely sure what I'd be into. I think I just want to test something out, see how it goes, you know?"

"Interesting," he murmured, and he leaned back in his seat, not taking his eyes off of me. I cocked an eyebrow at him.

"Is it?"

"It is," he agreed, a filthy little smile flicking up his lips. "I didn't take you for...well, I guess we'll find out what you are, won't we?"

"Guess we will," I agreed. "So, what do I do? Where do I start? Is there, like, somewhere I can go to find out about this stuff...?"

"There are meets most months," he explained, and he pulled his phone from his pocket, pulled up a page for me, and handed it over. "For people into this stuff. Usually just to hang out, but sometimes they put on special exhibitions for people like you. People who are interested to see everything that they can get out of the scene."

"Oh, how long till another one of them?" I asked, feeling a little crestfallen. I had been so into the idea of seeing where I could go with this, and it seemed like it was going to be a while before I could come out and actually enjoy it.

"Well, I'm the one who runs them," Tommy replied, leaning back in his seat with a broad grin on his face. "So, I'm pretty sure I can make it happen sooner rather than later."

My eyes widened. I knew that he was big in this city's sex scene, but this? This was a shock. I didn't know that I had managed to hook up with someone who pulled the strings in such a major way. But hey – if I could use it, I was sure as hell going to. I felt like I had already proved to him without a shadow of a doubt everything that I was willing to get up to in pursuit of pleasure, so he knew that I was far from some fair-weather pervert...

And so, I left it to him to pull everything together – he seemed enthused by the idea of introducing me to this world, and I was glad that I had someone I knew already in the scene so that they would be able to show me how to make sure I didn't make a damn fool of myself the moment I stepped through that door.

Within two weeks, he had sent me a formal invite to one of their performances – that's what he called them, his performances, like I was to be attending a live theatre event. I supposed, in some ways, I really was. After all, I knew that these were all performances, the same way that I performed for everyone that I'd slept with. The same way that I'd performed online in that livestream for everyone who had been watching me. There was something exciting about knowing that you didn't have to worry about a silly little thing like being yourself. You could just let go, have fun, and explore.

And that's just what I intended to do.

I think I changed my choice of outfit at least ten times before I was sure that I had something that would sell me the best. I had no clue exactly what I was looking for in this place – to dominate, to submit, both, something in between? I kept reminding myself, in the cab down to the hotel where this was to be taking place, that I didn't have to know going in. That I was showing up because I wanted to discover this part of myself.

Tommy was waiting for me by the time I arrived, dressed in a handsome formal suit – clearly the man behind all of this, and not afraid for everyone to know it. He offered me his arm and I took it, glad that I was to have some company tonight.

"You look lovely," he remarked. It was about the most PG-rated compliment that he had ever given me, as though he was making a point that this wasn't about the two of us – this was about me, me finding a chance to explore sides of myself that I had never touched on before.

"Are you nervous?" He asked. I nodded, as we made our way through the lobby. The receptionist locked eyes with me for a moment, and I wondered if she had any clue at all what was going on in their exhibition space. Did they have to hide it, make sure that nobody found out? Or did they want everyone to know?

"A little," I admitted. "I've never done anything like this before. It's...a lot."

"You're going to love it," he assured me, and we paused outside the large double doors that led into the main hall.

"You ready?" He asked, and I nodded, chewing my lip and hoping that he couldn't sense my toes curling with nerves inside my heels.

"Then let's do it," he replied, and he pushed open the door and let me inside.

And what I saw on the other side was enough to make my jaw drop.

I think the first thing that stunned me was the fact that there were so *many* people there. So many people who I wouldn't have looked at twice if I had passed them on the street – no, they seemed downright normal compared to what I'd expected. All of them seemed to be any natural person that I could have run into on any day out in the real world, but they were here, to enjoy this sensual night with me and the rest of the people we were going to share this with.

"Where do you want to start?" He asked me, leaning in a little closer to brush his lips oh-so-casually against my ear so that I could feel the overheated sensation of his breath against my skin. God, I still wanted him, still wanted him badly, but right now, I was distracted by everything else that was going on inside that room.

All around us, there were small stages, set up to show off the people performing on top of them – and what performances they were putting on, too. The one that drew my eye at once featured a man and a woman, her on her knees as she gazed up at him – he had a hand on her chin, tilting it up so that she had no choice but to look into his eyes. It seemed as though she wouldn't have wanted to be anywhere else right now, even if she had been able to. I didn't blame her. The focus in her gaze in that moment, the sureness of the way that she was staring at him, seemed like it was the only thing inside her right now.

"Can we go see what they're doing?" I asked him, and I nodded towards the two I had been staring at; he led me over there, and I followed behind him, hoping to God that I wasn't doing something silly or stupid. I knew that everyone here must have been able to tell that I was nothing more than an intruder in this land of theirs, but I needed to start somewhere, didn't I?

And so, start I did. A small crowd had circled around the stage that I was particularly interested in, and the way that the woman was staring at him was even more intense now that I was up-close and personal with all of it. I wanted nothing more than to feel what she was feeling at that moment – to feel the intensity of being wanted like that, of wanting in that way.

"Good girl," The man told her, and the sound of those words sent a long shiver down my spine. God, what was it about the way that he spoke to her that turned me on so much? It didn't make any sense to me, and yet, I couldn't deny how gorgeously sexy it was. His voice was cool, calm, confident and collected, and I adored the way that it sounded when he spoke to her.

"Thank you, sir," she breathed, and he ran his hand to the back of her head, his fingers wrapping around her hair so that he could pull her back sharply. Her eyes widened with excitement, and I could tell that she was savoring every moment of this. Every moment of what he could give to her.

"Open your mouth," he ordered, and she parted her lips at once – he pushed three fingers from his other hand into her mouth, and she sealed her lips around them and began to suck on them instantly. As though they were already well-practiced with this, with everything that it meant.

There was something almost painfully erotic about seeing that girl give herself to him like that. All she was doing was sucking and licking on his fingers, that was it, but it was more intense than if she had been down on her knees and blowing his cock in front of everyone in that moment. I knew that she must have been burning with want for him; even from the distance that I was standing, I could feel that coming off of her in waves.

I took another step forward, fascinated by what I was seeing. I didn't want to lose a single instant of this. I didn't know if I was ever going to get the chance to see something like this so close-up again, and I wanted to indulge myself with everything that came with it, all the ways that I could take it in. I was reminded of my hotel rendezvous a few days before, how hot it had been to be taken control of in that way, how good it had felt not to have to worry about anything other than just letting his want rush through me.

I didn't know if I would have been able to perform it like this for an audience, but I knew that I would have been pretty damn willing to try and find out. The thought of being watched as I gave myself over to someone like that, allowing a person to take full and utter control of me any way that they wanted to, was enough to send a hot, needy shiver down my spine.

He stirred his fingers in her mouth for a moment before he withdrew his hand once more, and I watched as she caught her breath, not taking her eyes off of him for a moment. I had to avert my gaze. I realized that I was breathing harder than I had been before, and I had to take a moment to control myself before I gave away in front of all of these people just how hot I found all of this.

"Would you like some privacy?" Tommy asked me, seeming to notice the change in my demeanor; I nodded, and, with an arm around my waist, he guided me to one of the rooms that ran along the side of the main hall, opening the door and gently moving me inside.

"Are you okay?" He asked me, softly, catching my face in his hand for a moment as he examined me carefully.

"I'm okay," I replied, hardly able to keep the smile off of my face. "I just...didn't expect to be so..."

I didn't know how to tell him what was going through my head, I didn't know how to express the want that had rushed upon me as soon as I had seen that woman in that way. I just wanted to be that girl, on her knees, consumed by the want that someone else had for her.

"It can be a lot to take in, the first time," he assured me, his voice careful, as though he was letting me come back down to Earth. I appreciated it. Honestly, I felt as though I was going to lose it if I didn't hold myself together as best I could right now. I could feel that deep, keening desire for something else inside of me, for something deeper and darker than I had ever experienced before.

"I really want to try something like that," I blurted out to him, and I managed to look up at him again – I had no idea what he was into, if this was even something that he would be able to handle, but I knew that I needed to feel it. Properly. Not just the control that the man I had been with in that hotel had taken from me, but something more intense than that.

He raised his eyebrows at me.

"Are you sure?" He asked, as he joined me on the small bench that ran around the outside of the room. I nodded. I felt like I was hypnotized, focused only on what I could find out next. I had already come so far in this journey of mine to uncover everything that I knew about myself; what was one more step? Just one more step forward to find out how it all unfolded?

"I know I am," I breathed, and I reached up to touch his face. "I want it to be you. I want you to show me..."

He rose to his feet once more. Something about the way he towered over me made my head spin. Even something as simple as that, as the mere difference in our height, was enough to make me feel cowed to him.

And I liked it.

"Wait here," he told me. "Don't move."

As if I was even thinking about it anyway. I stayed right where I was, not even twitching a muscle, as I waited for him to return. A few moments later, he did – and this time, he was carrying a small set of rope in his hand. Slim and red, I could already feel them biting into my skin before he had put them on me.

"Hold your hands up," he murmured, and I did as I was told at once. He slowly wrapped the rope around my wrists, the feeling of the fabric shocking and new as it caressed me softly. I didn't take my eyes off him. He was looking down at me as though he couldn't believe that this was really happening, that he was really going through with something like this.

"If you want to stop," he continued. "You say the word *red.* Okay? You got that?"

"I got that," I breathed. He tightened the rope around my wrists properly. I gasped at the feeling of it tying into my skin. Something about that restriction, about knowing that I couldn't pull myself loose, made me shiver with anticipation.

"How far do you want to go?" He asked me. I shook my head. I had no idea how I was meant to answer that question, no idea what I was meant to say.

"Just...show me where it starts," I replied. "Please. I want to feel what that woman was feeling back there..."

"I'll see what I can do," he murmured, and I could tell from the glint in his eyes that he was already excited at the thought of what he was going to bring to me next. My heart was slamming against my ribs and I was barely able to catch my breath as I waited for him to do whatever he was going to do next. Slowly, he peeled back my fingers, so that my palms were held upright to him in front of me.

I noticed a small whip that he had brought into the room with him – he had laid it on one of the seats surrounding the walls, and he now plucked it, held it in his hands for a moment. The leather glinted almost cruelly in the dark, and I had to bite my lip to keep from letting out a moan of excitement.

"Do you know what this is?" He asked me. I nodded.

"I do."

"And do you know what I want to do with it?"

"No, I don't."

"I want to hurt you," he replied, and he trailed the very tip of it over the upturned spread of my hands, sending a shiver all the way down my wrists, across my arms, over my shoulders, and down my back. In this state, it felt like every tiny little touch was enough to light me on fire.

"I am going to strike your palms," he explained, a dark want starting to cloud the edge of his voice. "And you're going to count out every single blow with me. You understand?"

"I understand," I breathed. He brought the whip back, and landed a short, sharp strike on my hands. The shock of it made me jolt, but at the same time – I liked it. I liked the way that it felt. I liked the way it felt when it caressed me like that, when I saw the soft pink mark turn up on my hands.

"How was it?" He asked me, reaching down to grip my face in his hand. I shook my head. I didn't know what I was meant to say, but I knew that I wanted more.

"Again," I breathed. And, without another word, he brought it down on me once more.

This time, I let out a cry – the shock of it was almost more than I could take, but I loved it, ached for it, and needed it. My entire system responded as he continued to hurt me, and I marveled at how magical it could feel right now. How wonderful it was to be hurt by this man, even though I knew that he wanted nothing more than to pleasure me.

He laid down five more blows on my hands, and I managed to contain myself, pressing my lips together so that I didn't make any hint of noise as he did so. Oh, he knew just what he was doing to me, just what he wanted from me – the sound of that leather biting into my skin was enough to send shockwaves through my whole system, and I had to clamp my legs together to keep myself from moaning with every touch.

He pulled the whip back once more, seeming to sense that I'd taken as much as I was going to be able to manage. His eyes were pinned to mine, looking for a reaction, and I was breathing hard, I couldn't hide it.

"How is it?" He asked. I tipped my head back, locked my eyes to his.

"So good," I groaned, and I pressed my thighs together again, trying to relieve some of the tension that had built there between my legs. I wanted nothing more than to get some relief, but I wasn't sure if I was allowed to ask for it or if I had to wait for him to gift it to me.

"Are you wet right now?" He asked. His voice had taken on a darker, deeper air now, something that made me nod along at once.

"So wet," I moaned, and he moved to put his hand between my legs, grazing his fingers against the outside of my panties. I gasped.

"Get up," he ordered, and he pulled me to my shaky feet and pushed me back down over the bench at the other side of the room, so that my dress heaved up around my hips and exposed me – he reached between my thighs and ripped off my panties, reaching around to stuff them into my mouth. The shock of feeling my own muskiness between my lips thrilled me, and I groaned against the soft fabric between my lips.

"I want to fuck you now," he told me, and he paused for a moment, giving me that instant that I might have needed to stop things before they went any further. But in truth, I didn't want them to stop. I didn't want to let this slip through my fingers. I wanted him to fuck me, hard and fast, I wanted him to make me come around his cock, and I wanted to feel myself finally get the relief that I needed so badly.

I heard the rip of a condom behind me, and, with my bound hands pushing me up off the bench, I arched my back to give him all the access that he needed to move inside of me. A few moments later, I felt the pressure of his cock at my entrance, and then, at last, his fullness sliding into me once more.

I groaned against the panties that were wadded into my mouth as he plunged into me for the first time. The restraints around my wrists and the fullness of his cock in my pussy was almost more than I could take — the throbbing pain still laid across my hands as the pleasure echoed all the way up and through my body mixed together, creating something seductive and sensual and impossibly sexy. I pushed myself back to meet him, needing more, needing all that he could give me. I wasn't sure that I would ever be able to have enough of this, this tantalizing mix of a man that I desired with such painful want and the control that I had to give him to let this happen.

"Fuck, yes," he growled, and he grabbed my hips and started to slam into me deeper than before. This wasn't the sensual sex that I'd shared with him and his man; this was something else entirely, something more intense than that. Something that seemed to wipe all logical thought from my mind and boil me down to the barest minimum of everything that I could wrap my head around.

"God, you look so good like that," he told me, and all I could do was let out another muffled moan to tell him just how good he felt, too. Anyone from that party outside could have walked in on us at any moment, and there would have been nothing I could do to hide how exposed I was right now. And for some reason, the thought of that fucking thrilled me. If he'd wanted to take me out there, show me off for everyone to see, let everyone in there take me in all bound and gagged and fucked like that, there would have been nothing I could do to stop it.

And it was that feeling of complete and utter helplessness that finally took me where I needed to go. I felt it, the same thing that I had been sure that woman had been feeling when she had been sucking on the fingers of her man the way she was— the certainty that all that mattered in the world was pleasing this person, giving yourself to them any way that you possibly could. I arched my back and pushed my hips back to meet him, hard, letting him drive himself into me over and over again, filling me roughly with his full length as the sound of our flesh coming together filled my ears.

I wanted to reach back and tell him to go even deeper, but he had bound me, gagged me, left me with nothing but the hope that he would be able to give me everything that I wanted right now. I could feel the breath overheating in my lungs, the corners of my vision starting to get blurry as I felt myself cresting – cresting – cresting – and then-

When the orgasm hit, I was glad that he had gagged me. Glad that he had quietened me down. Because the pleasure was so intense that I knew I would have screamed at the top of my lungs if he hadn't been there to shut me up. He drove himself deep, one last time, inside of me, and held himself there for a long moment, letting my pussy contract and clench around his length over and over again.

Finally, I felt his cock twitch inside of me, as I slumped forward on to the bench, trying to gather myself after the shock of that near-painful pleasure had started to subside. He pulled himself out of me, and my body slipped down to the floor, my pussy throbbing with relief as the last vestiges of that orgasm rushed through my system.

And I knew, in that moment, that this would be far from the last time that I ever came to a place like this – and far from the last time that I ever got to indulge myself in some power play like this kind.

Chapter 11

F, Solo, Shower Fantasy Masturbation

Waking up in my bed, all alone, with nothing but the tenderness of my pussy after the deep fucking that I had taken the night before – well, it was enough to make any girl feel glad that she had some time to herself to recover.

I still couldn't quite believe that I had really done all of that. Really gone to that party, really let myself get tied up and whipped, and been so helplessly wet from all of it that I had allowed the man who had done it to me to fuck me afterwards.

I snuggled into the sheets, letting out a happy little sigh. Hard to believe that I was still the person I was when I had moved into this place, right? Hard to believe that someone like me could have hidden this side of herself for so long. I felt like I was starting to come into myself in the way that I had always been meant to, started to embrace something deep and longing inside of me that had been waiting to come out for longer than I would have cared to admit.

But what else was there for me to explore? And what did I really want for myself if I had come to the end of the journey that I had been on that had led me here in the first place? I had no idea what this looked like when it was all over, whether it would ever truly be over, or if I would constantly be finding ways to evolve myself, my desire, the things that I wanted and the things that I never knew I needed.

I sighed as I lifted myself out of bed, went for a hot shower to wash the remnants of last night off of me. There were the barest hints of pink marks around my wrists from where he had bound me the night before, and I didn't mind one little bit. In fact, I wore it as a badge of honor, the way that I had been able to keep up with him and endure everything that he had put me through. I knew that I would soon be back for more, to find out what else I could take, and I loved the thought of pushing myself to another high – maybe even putting myself in the position of that woman who had been on her knees and taking everything her man had been giving her. Maybe there was something to be said for that, too.

The warm water of the shower rushed over my body, massaging out the kinks in my muscles as it went, and I smiled as it soothed me. Honestly, I wished that there was someone else with me in here right now, even though I know this alone time to recover was also feeling nice. I just felt like, the more sex that I had, the more that I craved it, the more that I found myself going deeper into my desires, the more they seemed to stir up. I had to laugh now, thinking about all the ways that I had tried to tell myself that I just didn't feel the same desire that other women did when I had been with my ex – looking back, I could tell that it had been nothing more than my own attempts to cover up the fact that it was *him* who was the problem, who had always been the problem.

I let my fingers trace down my body, till they came to a halt between my legs – the warm water over my skin had already gotten my clit throbbing with want, and I knew that I had to give in to it. I rubbed my fingers down either side of my clit, slowly, in a V-shape, feeling the pressure of the skin pulling taut around me for just the barest moment. I gasped, leaned my head back against the shower, and did my best to picture someone else's hand between my legs instead.

I could almost imagine it, and almost feel their fingers in place of my own – no, their fingers guiding mine, showing me just how I should touch myself. I moaned softly as I imagined this man slowly tracing his fingers over my clit, taking his time, making sure that he didn't rush himself. Making sure that he was going to make me wait.

He didn't have a face, but he had a body – a warm, strong body that I could feel all pressed up against mine, holding me close, touching me and telling me every way he knew how that he wanted me. I wished that I could feel the hardness of his cock against my ass, but for now, I would just have to stick with the thought of his fingers, teasing me, tracing me, caressing me. Making sure that I knew just how deeply I belonged to him, and just how uninterested he was in letting me escape from his touch.

Before I knew it, my back was arched, and I was thrusting against my hand harder than before. The pressure on my clit was intense, and I could already feel the orgasm starting to stir and build inside of me. God, I can't believe how bad I always want this now and how much I feel like I need it – I had to know what happened next, how it would feel to climax like this. The water was running down my body, between my breasts, down between my legs, as though it was tracing the shape of the pleasure that I was marking out on myself...

"Oh," I groaned, as it finally flooded through me. The relief of that orgasm made my knees tremble and my entire body shake for a moment. I had to hold my hand still to keep myself from tumbling to the ground on the spot. Reaching to grasp for the edge of the shower head, I held on for dear life, pulling it down between my legs so that the hot water could continue to massage my clit as I came, helplessly, the wetness meshing with the water so that I couldn't think about anything else in the world at all.

By the time that I had come back down to Earth, I realized that I actually needed to clean myself up and get myself off to work for the day. Sometimes, the pleasure became so much that I couldn't think about anything but how much I wanted to come, and come, and come again, until everything fell away, and the only thing left was the delicious and implacable joy that my body could bring me.

But a woman couldn't live on orgasms alone. Even as much as I might have wanted to. So, I did the responsible thing, got myself cleaned up for work, and headed out the door to make sure that I would be there on time. I promised myself that I wasn't going to let these new desires of mine run me too ragged.

I flashed myself a smile as I got ready in the mirror for my day at work. I was sure that this was the very best way to start off any working week. And I intended to make sure that it was the best I'd ever had.

Chapter 12

F/F, Oral Sex, Public, Femdom

"Hey, could you check that the till is all sorted?" Dinah called to me, as she headed back into the kitchen to make sure that everything was tidied away for the night.

"Yeah, sure," I promised her, and I hummed to myself as I headed round the desk to do as I was told. I was in a good mood today, probably thanks to the delicious orgasm I had given myself before I had left the house. Note to self – I needed to start doing that more often. If there was anything that would get me out of bed with a smile on my face, it was knowing that I could make myself come before I had to step out of the front door.

I could feel eyes on me as I cashed out the till, and I looked up to see Dinah, one of the girls that I had been on shift with that afternoon, watching me from where she stood. I smiled at her, furrowed my brow.

"What is it?" I asked, trying to contain the little chuckle of surprise that I felt at being the center of her attention like this. Dinah had always been one of those girls who very much kept to herself, and she never did much talking to the rest of us unless it was for something about work.

"Nothing," she remarked. "It's just that there's...something different about you, I think."

"Different in a good way, or in a bad way?" I wondered. She chuckled.

"A good way, don't worry," she replied. "I wouldn't bring it up if it wasn't a good way."

"Hmm, glad to hear it," I replied, and I couldn't help but smile right back at her. She had a nice smile, warm and friendly, but usually it was aimed at the customers instead of the other people she worked with.

"Something changed recently?" She asked. She was trying to keep her voice casual, but I could tell that she was in anything but that kind of headspace right now. Was she curious about me? I was flattered - I couldn't remember the last time that she had shown any interest in any of us, not really, and the thought of that coming down to land on me made me happier than it should. If there was one thing that I had learned that I thrived on in these last few months, it was attention – especially attention from people who I didn't think really cared that much about me before they handed it over.

"I suppose it has," I replied with a shrug, trying to keep my voice casual. "I split with my fiancé recently. Maybe that's what you're noticing."

"Oh, sorry to hear it," she replied, the corners of her mouth turning down with concern. I shook my head and laughed.

"Oh, really, nothing to be sorry about," I assured her. "I'm much better off without him."

"I find that's true of most men," she replied bluntly, and I couldn't help but let out a surprised laugh.

"You had a hard time with them?" I asked, and she shook her head.

"Not with them," She countered. "Just...about them."

"What do you mean?" I wondered aloud. She had always been so secretive, and I knew that my curiosity was unlikely to be sated again if I missed the chance to do it now.

"My mom was always trying to set me up with boys she thought I would like," she explained, shaking her head.

"And it didn't work out?" I asked with interest. She chuckled and shook her head.

"No, because I was a lesbian and I knew it and she just wouldn't accept it about me," she replied. She sounded almost amused by it now, like she was glad that she could just laugh about something so horrible. I raised my eyebrows in surprise. For all the things that she had kept secret, this was about the very last thing that I had expected to come out of her mouth.

"Oh, shit, you're not one of them, are you?" She remarked, raising her eyebrows at me.

"One of who?"

"One of those people who's going to try and convert me, or something," she replied, warily. I shook my head at once.

"No, no, never," I promised her. "I'm just – I didn't know that about you, that's all."

"Oh, trust me, I didn't know it about myself for a long time either," she replied, with a sly smile. "Sorry. Didn't mean to dump it on you if you weren't ready to hear it."

"It's fine, really," I promised her. Honestly, now that she had said it out loud, there was a part of me that wanted to find out what else she had going on – a part of me that couldn't help but notice how cute she happened to be, with that cropped dark hair, those big green eyes, that slightly crooked nose that brought real character to her face.

"So trust me, I totally understand living in a world without men," She replied. "And how much better it can be for your sanity to keep them out of your head."

"Agreed," I laughed, as I finished cashing up the till. I noticed that the soles of my feet were starting to prickle, and I knew it had everything to do with this new revelation that I had just found out about her. I was drawn to her, intrigued in a way that I hadn't been before. It had been a while since I had last been with a woman, and honestly, though I had been picturing a man when I had been touching myself in the bathroom that morning, I wouldn't have minded one little bit if it had been Dinah in there with me.

"How are you finding being single?" She asked me. Her voice was carefully casual, but I was sure that she was trying to open up a few doors, figure out a few things that she clearly suspected about me. I could play along with that. I wanted to find out what she would do when she discovered that I was nowhere near as heterosexual as she had always thought I'd been.

"It's a lot of fun," I replied, tucking a strand of hair back behind my ear as she came to lean on the counter to talk to me. It was just the two of us in that place together, the shutters half-pulled down to make sure that nobody from the street outside would make the mistake of wandering in and thinking we were open, and there was something both peaceful and a little tense about being alone here with her.

"Oh, yeah?"

"Yeah, for sure," I replied, trying to ignore the urge to slide my hand across the counter and just lightly rest it on hers. It would be so fun to see what she would do – but we worked together, I didn't want to be the one to come out here and make things awkward. She was likely just making a little polite conversation before she returned to go back to business, get home for the night.

But there was something about the way that she was looking at me that made me wonder if there might have been something more to it.

"Getting to find out a lot about myself," I continued, pushing my hand through my hair again. God, I was flirting, wasn't I? There was no denying it. I could have sat here and played the fool, made like I didn't know what on earth she was talking about, but I was flirting with her and I was hoping that she was going to pick up on it sooner rather than later.

"Like what?" She asked, gazing up at me with those gorgeous green eyes, not breaking my gaze for a second.

"Like that I might not be..." I began, and then I trailed off, shook my head, laughed.

"No, no, I can't talk about that," I finished up playfully, and she raised her eyebrows.

"Well, now you have to tell me."

"Do I?"

"It's the rules."

"Well," I murmured, flicking my tongue out over my lips. I could see her gaze flicker down to meet it for just a split second, and I had to bite back a little giggle of amusement. Had it always been this much fun to flirt with people, and I had just been way too repressed to notice it?

"That I'm not as straight as I thought I was," I confessed, lowering my eyes for a moment, not sure how she would take this revelation. But when I looked up again, I found her smiling back at me, leaning a little closer over the counter.

"Oh, I already knew that," she murmured, and I raised my eyebrows in surprise.

"What do you mean?"

"You always gave me that vibe," she replied, with a shrug. "I've never been wrong about a girl yet, even when they're not out of the closet."

"I don't know if I'm out or in right now," I confessed, and she reached over to my side of the counter, pushed the stray strand of hair that had been bugging me away from my face, and then let her fingers trace down my skin for a moment. Her touch was practiced, and it was clear it was far from the first time that she had ever touched a woman like this.

"It doesn't matter," she murmured. "You're wherever you need to be."

"I think I need to be...with you," I admitted. I had thought that I was the one in total charge of this conversation and how it was going to unfold, but the more time that passed, the clearer it became that this had been her intention from the start, and I was just lucky to get caught up in it right now.

"Oh, yeah?" She prompted me softly. She wanted to hear everything that I had to say about this, and honestly, I wanted to tell her - I wanted to tell her everything that was on my mind right now, everything that had popped into it the moment that I had felt her fingers on my skin.

But why tell her, when I could just show her?

I leaned forward and planted my lips against hers for the first time. God, she tasted good − caramel, vanilla, something sweet and spiced and deep. I wanted nothing more than to just linger in that moment a little longer, feel the pressure of her lips against mine, let the thrill of it roll through me.

But before I could even catch my breath, she came around to my side of the counter to kiss me properly. Pressing her body against mine, she grasped my chin in her hand as she pushed her tongue into my mouth; dominant, controlling, passionate. I groaned and moved myself back against her, running my hand down her arm, feeling the strength of it as she held me right there in front of her. I was whatever she wanted me to be right now, whatever she needed of me, and she seemed to know that clearer than anything in the world.

The way she touched me reminded me of the night that I had spent at the kink party – she might have been a woman, but that didn't mean that she wouldn't take complete and total control where she wanted to. She shoved her thigh between my legs to spread them, gave me something to grind on while she continued to kiss me. At once, and as though on her command, I started to move against her, sliding my body against hers hungrily, needing more, wanting more, willing to do anything that I could to make sure that it happened.

"Hmm, see, I could tell you always liked girls," she murmured in my ear, her voice cocky with the clear enjoyment of the way that I was reacting to her right now. I wondered if this was something that she enjoyed, getting with women who were only just starting to explore the possibility of a lesbian journey in their own life. If she wanted to show me how things were done, then I was sure as hell going to let her...

She slipped her hand to the front of my pants as I pressed myself against her thigh, and slowly inched the zipper down until she could push her fingers into my panties properly. I was already swollen and wet, my pussy aching for a release like the one I had given myself in the shower this morning, and I was obsessed with how gentle she was, how careful – taking her sweet-ass time, making sure that she took in every gasp and every moan that I let out.

"You're so wet for me already," she teased me lightly, clearly enjoying the response that I had to her as she slowly massaged my clit with two fingers. I wanted to feel her inside me – no, I wanted her mouth on my pussy. No, I couldn't tell what I actually desired right now, only that I ached for more, as much as she could give me, as much as she was willing to share.

She hitched me up onto the counter behind me, pulled down my pants and my underwear, and shoved my legs apart roughly – sinking to her knees, she didn't take her eyes off of me as she went to sink her mouth against the inside of my thigh, making my legs vibrate with a desperate want as I watched her in action.

"Oh, you like that?" She asked, playing innocent, as she bared her teeth and bit down on my thigh once more, the sensitive skin practically lighting up at her experienced touch. How could this woman ever have had anything to do with a man, ever, in her whole life? It seemed ridiculous to even think about now – but, as she skimmed her lips towards my pussy at last, I wasn't thinking about much else in the world but how much I wanted them planted against me properly.

She grazed her mouth over my clit for the briefest moment, and I tipped my head back on the counter and let out a long groan. I knew that anyone walking the streets outside could probably hear me, and God only knew if the CCTV was still on in here and catching us in the act. Maybe I wanted it to be. Maybe I wanted to be seen like this with her, to be touched and pleasured for everyone to watch. I glanced up in the direction of one of the cameras that I couldn't remember if I had switched off yet, and wondered if there was someone on the other end of that line, watching me, taking me in, admiring the way I looked with having a woman between my legs who was willing to make me come.

She swirled her tongue around my clit before she drew it into her mouth properly, slowly rolling it between her lips like she was taking her time to savor every inch of me. And God, did it feel good – the pressure was already enough to make my legs tremble a little, and I had to bite my lip hard to keep from begging her for more. I knew that she would do this at her own pace and nobody else's, and as tempting as it was to just start grinding on her face to show her how much I was enjoying her attention, I knew that I had to be more careful than that. I knew that I had to let her show me how it was done.

"You taste perfect," she murmured, as she pulled back for a moment to admire my soaked pussy – her eyes flicked up to meet mine, and she smiled, the grin spreading over her face for a second before she dived back in to plant her mouth against my pussy once more.

This time, I couldn't hold myself back. I clamped my thighs around her head, squeezing her in place, not willing to let her go. I needed to come right now – I needed to feel myself finish here. I reached down, grasped her head, ran my fingers through her hair, and focused on the way that her soft mouth caressed me, curious to find out every way that I would react to every single little thing that was going on down there.

Her tongue lapped all the way from my slit to my clit and back down again, drenching me with a mixture of her saliva and my own juices; every now and then, she would pull back for a moment to catch her breath, and she would steal a look up at me to make sure that I was still desperate for her. And, once she was satisfied that I couldn't even come close to controlling myself, she would press herself back in, her tongue circling my clit once more as she worshipped every inch of my pussy with her lips and her tongue.

She teased it out of me for a hell of a long time, making me wait and making me suffer just a little before she gave me what I wanted more than anything in the world. As soon as she sensed the inside of my thighs starting to twitch, she seemed to give in to actually letting me come, lapping at my clit in slow, quick motions that made my body begin to spiral into that place of endless, impossible pleasure.

"Ohhh," I groaned, and I balled my hand to a fist in her hair, tightening my grip on her, not even caring if I was hurting her – all that mattered was getting where I needed to go right now, and nothing was going to stop me from going there. I was pushing back against her, my hips seeming to move almost of their own accord, my pussy starting to pulse and clench – I gritted my teeth, let my head fall back, held my breath, as I finally, finally felt it surge through me.

When I came, I swear that I left my body for a moment in time. Because there was no way that I could feel this good and still be the person that I had always thought I was before. Stars prickled behind my eyes and I felt my legs starting to tremble, that helpless, hopeless giving-in to the way that it felt and the way that I wanted to keep feeling. I groaned, held her in place, hands meshed in her hair, as I thrust my hips back at her, over and over again until everything had fallen from my head except the need for more.

By the time that I finally pushed her back from my pussy, there was a cocky-ass smile on her face, and I could tell that she was pleased with how she had made me come. She rose to her feet, kissed me once more, her tongue dancing around mine for a moment so that I could taste myself on her lips. I was still panting, my legs still shaking, and she seemed to be enjoying every single one of my reactions.

"We should close up together more often," she told me, and I giggled. I didn't know what to say. All I knew was that she was correct – and that I would be doing everything in my power to make sure that I got to spend as much time with her in the future as I possibly could.

Chapter 13

F/M/M/M/M, Gangbang, Anal, Double Penetration

I hovered outside the theatre, looking at my watch, trying to seem as innocuous as possible. Which was pretty damn hard, given that I was lurking outside of a porno cinema, and waiting to slip inside once I had built up the courage to actually step through the door.

I couldn't believe that I was going through with this. The same question had been thrumming in my head over and over again, until I couldn't think about anything else — that I was really going through with it, that I was really doing it, that I was really, really, really about to slide into a place full of perverts as depraved as I was and give myself over to the helpless, hopeless want that we could all share together, once and for all.

It had been nearly a week since my hook-up with Dinah at the café, and I had been craving for something new to set my nerves on fire; this had popped up in my memory, some vague, distant picture of people going out to some cinema together where they would all watch the same porno movie and mess around with each other as they did so. An old-fashioned idea, one that I was sure I had gotten from a lifetime ago, but when I found out that there was an adults-only theater not far from my new place, I felt like I didn't have any other choice but to come down here and check it out.

I didn't even know the film that they were showing – just knew that if I got the nerve to go through that door, then I would be surrounded by people as horny as I was. People who were as desperate for the new thrills and spills of an erotic adventure like I had been these last few months. My people, in other words – and I wanted to find out what they had in store for me.

Finally, I managed to gather myself enough to walk to the desk, where a bored-looking young woman was handing out tickets. She barely looked at me through the slightly grimy glass, and I handed my money over to her at once. She slid a ticket back, and jerked her head inside the building. I didn't need telling twice. Before she could say another word, I went inside, and found myself in my very first porno theater.

It was actually cuter inside than I had expected it to be. In my mind, I had been ready to walk into a group of masturbating middle-aged men who were so horny they couldn't even hold it till they were inside the cinema. But instead, I saw a couple of guys, one close to my age, readying themselves to head in. I caught the eye of the younger one, flashed him a smile, and he eyed me for a moment before he turned his back to head inside the theater.

I followed him inside, the movie had already started to play, and my eyes were drawn to the heaving mounds of flesh on the screen, the way the actress moaned loudly as the porn star in front of us gave her a good dicking-down. God, I wish that could have been me — getting fucked so hard I couldn't see straight. Especially for an audience. Even better, right?

I looked around, to see maybe two dozen men filling out the rest of the theater around me. They were all sitting distantly apart from each other, but I could feel the atmosphere shift as soon as I walked into the room. I was the only woman there, and the thought of that thrilled me — the thought of being the only girl nasty and depraved enough to risk a place like this made my stomach twist in excitement.

I slipped down into a seat at the edge of the aisle. The smell of sex and want was heavy in the air, and it thrilled me to think of how much desire was pulsing around me right now. I glanced around at the other man down the row from me — he was rubbing his cock over his pants, clearly already hard at the sight of the screen in front of him, and when his eyes locked with mine, he paused for a moment, raised his eyebrows, as though he was asking me to come down there to join him.

Amongst the groaning and grunting and grinding on the screen in front of me, I knew that I couldn't say no. I didn't want to. I slipped a few seats down to join him, and he grasped my hand and drew it to his cock — he didn't bother waiting around, watching as my fingers rubbed at his impressive bulge. God, he was big — and hard already, too. I had brought condoms with me, just in case, and it was tempting...

I slipped his zipper down, and then slid my hand into his boxers, sliding my fingers over the top of his hard-on and watching as he tipped his head back and groaned with need. I bit my lip, stole a whiff of his smell, that deep, masculine scent that brought me to places that I couldn't escape any longer. I crossed my legs tight, letting the delicious warmth shiver up my system and control me.

"Fuck," he growled, as I took his cock out of his pants and started to stroke him properly. I knew that the other men in the cinema around us must have noticed what we were up to, and I wondered if they cared – if they were watching us more than they were watching the film in front of them, by now. I loved the thought of it, the thought of being a more erotic prospect than what was going on in the picture we were meant to be watching together.

His cock was so big, it was hard to fit my hand all the way around it – I slowly stroked up, up and down, using the few drops of pre-cum on his tip to moisten him so that I could jerk him off properly. He tipped his head back and leaned it on the chair behind him, closing his eyes while I pleasured him. I watched the tension in his face, realized that I didn't even know his name – and that I didn't care to find it out, either. All I wanted was to touch him, caress him, watch him lose himself to me and the way that I made him feel, and that was just what I intended to do.

I shifted towards him, sliding my other hand down his leg. I wanted to climb on top of him and feel his cock inside of me, but I didn't know if that would be breaking the etiquette in this place. Could I ask him? He opened his eyes again, looked at me, and I flicked my tongue over my bottom lip, telling him any way that I could that I wanted more, if he was willing to give it to me.

And, thank God, he was. He grabbed me by the hips and swung me up and on top of him, looking deep into my eyes with his blazing blue ones – the desire was so intense that I nearly swooned on the spot, but I managed to hold his gaze and look right back at him.

"I want you to fuck me," I moaned to him, theatrically. If he had come here for a show, then I was going to make sure that he got it – well, him, and everyone else who had come down here tonight, too.

I pushed a condom into his hand and watched as he quickly sheathed himself, and then pulled aside my panties so that I could ride him properly – I had only worn a skirt to this thing, not wanting anything to get in the way of the pleasure that I wanted to indulge in, and it didn't take long till I had pushed myself down on top of his hard cock.

He was even bigger than I had thought, the dark cloaking his hugeness, and I had to grip the backs of the velvet seats to grind down on him properly. His head was tipped back, his eyes starting to glaze, as though he could hardly believe that this was actually happening – as though he just wanted to lose himself to the pleasure that I was giving him. This was likely the last thing that he had expected, but that didn't mean that I wasn't going to show him just how much he deserved it.

I rocked my hips back and forward slowly, taking my time, getting used to the feeling of his enormous cock inside of me. My pussy was stretched to its very limits to take him in, but it felt perfect – just like the huge-dicked porn star on the screen in front of us, he was filling me the way I wanted to be filled. I tossed my hair over my shoulder, and I could feel more eyes on us – people watching us, checking to see what the live show was and if it had more to offer than the pre-recorded one they'd been watching up until this point.

I closed my eyes as I began to move up and down on top of him, until I sensed something in front of me – I opened them once more, and I couldn't help but smile when I saw the guy that had been there when I had walked in looking at me. Seemed like he just couldn't resist the thought of getting a little more out of me yet, huh?

I beckoned him forward, as the man below me began to thrust up and into my pussy. He was taking it hard, rough, showing me just how well he could fuck, and I wanted to take more. I was greedy for it. I reached out as the man behind us stood up, grabbed his jeans and pulled him forward – and I watched as his eyes widened with surprise as I unzipped his pants and began to stroke off his already-hard cock.

"Suck it," he moaned to me, as he grasped the back of my head to push it towards his cock. I flicked my gaze up to meet his, playing innocent, even though I had another cock fucking my pussy at this very moment. I let him guide me towards his hard-on, and swirled my tongue around his tip before I took him in deep, all the way, letting him push up to the hilt into my mouth.

The man who was fucking me moaned loudly, and I knew that he must have been enjoying the show that I was putting on as much as the one who I was blowing happened to be right now. He slipped his cock all the way down my throat for a moment, and held it there, clearly testing how far I could take this before I'd have to pull back and catch a breath, but I didn't even flinch. I could feel my eyes starting to water, but I ignored it, showing him that I could take everything from him that he could give me.

By the time he slipped back from my mouth, I glanced around, and realized that a small crowd had gathered to watch us. The rest of the men who had been in the theater were surrounding us right now. Most of them were jerking off, the rest rubbing themselves over their pants, and the shock of seeing so many boys all gathered around me, all focused on everything that I was doing for them, was enough to make me push down on the cock below me even harder, and feast on the one in front of me with even more passion than I had before.

He slammed himself into my pussy, so hard it nearly hurt, but I didn't care. I just wanted all that he could give to me, all that all of them could give to me. I had never felt hotter than in that moment, surrounded by men who desired me and couldn't get enough of me, surrounded by lust that was all directed at me and me alone.

The younger man pushed himself into my mouth again, and I moved my head back and forth on his cock frantically, so much so that saliva started to drip down my chin and over my neck. I was a mess, but I loved it, loved everything about it. I hadn't come down here to play the good girl and make like I didn't want to give myself over to this, did I? I had come down here because I'd wanted to meet other people who were just like me, other people who were willing to let the sheer lust pulse through them and take control. That was what mattered.

The fullness was starting to wipe everything else out of my memory, just like it had done when I had been with two men for the first time. But this was different. This was less sensual, more purely physical – everyone who was here had come down to this place because they wanted to let loose and have some fun, and I was going to show them just how much fun they could have when I was around.

I could already feel the orgasm starting to brew inside of me, and I grabbed the hand of the man who was fucking me and pulled it to my clit. He started rubbing hard, nothing tender about it, as he filled me hard and fast and over and over. Soon, the man at my mouth was matching the very same pace, and I let myself get lost to it, the feeling of being taken by two cocks at once was enough to push me to where I needed to go...

When I came, a flood of wetness shot from my pussy and all over his cock, his pants, the seat around me. I clenched myself around him, massaging him mercilessly with my pussy, and he groaned and held me on top of him for a long moment as he finished as well. It didn't take long till the one who was fucking my mouth drew back just far enough to give me warning, and then shot a jet of sperm over my lips and tongue and into my mouth. I dived back on to his cock to make sure that I could suck up every last drop of it once and for all, not wanting to miss a thing.

The three of us practically crumpled into each other as we got lost to the pleasure that we were giving to each other – I was distantly aware of the calls of encouragement and approval from the men who were around us, and the sound of the fucking that was still going on on the screen in front of us, but I knew that none of it would come close to the show that I had managed to put on for them.

But God, there was something more that I needed, too. Those two men might have been spent, but I wanted something else – something more. I managed to lift myself off of the man that I had just come all over, my legs shaking, and looked to the men who were standing around me. All that I could see was a parade of cocks that needed my attention, cocks that I wanted to give my lust and my love to.

"Who's next?" I demanded, as I quickly unbuttoned the top of my dress to show off my tits – I couldn't remember a time in my life when I had felt more powerful than this, more wanted. Their eyes were all over me, taking me in with a hunger that I had never seen before in my life. I reached for the one closest to me, a man a little younger than I was, and brought his hand to one of my bare breasts – he grabbed and squeezed it like it was the first tit that he'd ever had his hands on in his life. I hoped it was. I felt like a fucking sex goddess, and I wanted these men to worship me as though they were never going to get a show as good as this one again.

He moved towards me, kissed me hard, his hands scrambling all over my body like he was trying to make sure that all of this was real. I grasped his head, pushed him back so I could look deep into his eyes.

"Fuck me," I told him, and I grabbed another condom from my pocket and shoved it into his hand. He spun me around, pushed me down so that my ass was hanging out over the edge of the aisle and my pussy was fully on display to him. Around me, I could still see those men watching me, needing me, their eyes all over me as they imagined what it would be like when they got their turn with me. Well, I had plenty of time for everyone here – as long as that movie was still playing, then I still had all the hours that I needed to give them everything that they had been longing for when they had first come to this place.

I felt his fingers toy with my messy pussy, the wetness that was still leaking down my thighs making his fingers silky-smooth. And then, to my surprise, I felt him...I felt him inch a little higher.

I gasped as I felt his finger test the ring of my ass. I had never been fucked there before in my life, but it wasn't because I had some great problem with it. It had just never crossed my mind to try it before, usually because I wanted my pussy fucked before anything else. But right now, my slit was a little sore from the pounding that it had taken from the man I had just ridden, and I wouldn't have minded a little relief for the time being...

His finger slipped just an inch inside of me, and I gasped. God, it felt...good. I was surprised to find how easy it was for me to allow him to touch me like that, how delicious it seemed for his finger to push deeper and deeper inside of me. Before I knew it, he had another one, spreading my ass open as he allowed me to push back on to his hand like the needy little slut that I was.

"You want me to fuck you in the ass?" He asked me, loud enough for everyone around us to hear. I knew that, if I wanted him to keep going, then I was going to have to admit in front of all of these people that I wanted nothing more than to get my asshole filled – the dirtiest and sluttiest of acts, right here in the middle of this public theater surrounded by men who I had never met before in my life and who I would never meet again, either.

"Yes," I groaned. I couldn't believe I was agreeing to this. I knew that, after this, I would have gone to some place that I would never be able to come back from – gone to some desirous, sex-drunken spot in my mind that I was going to have to stick out at from this moment on. I didn't have a choice. But, as I felt his fingers push inside my tight asshole, I knew that there was no way that I could turn him down, either.

Slowly, he pulled his fingers out of my ass, and slipped the condom over his erection. I glanced over my shoulder – I couldn't tell much about his size from where

I was right now, but I knew that he couldn't be small as soon as I felt his head pressing against my virgin ass.

He popped past my entrance, and I had to inhale deeply to stop the pain from getting the better of me. But it only took a few seconds till I could let it rush through me, and I allowed the relief of his cock slowly moving into me to push everything else from my mind. I could feel the long breath out that he released as he moved all the way to the hilt inside of me, everyone around us practically holding their breath as though they were waiting to see if I could take a cock in my last virgin hole as well as I had already shown that I could in my others.

"Fuck, you're tight," he murmured, and he sank his hands into my ass to spread me a little wider open, making sure that I was totally available for him. I glanced over my shoulder and bit my lip, telling him every way that I knew how that I wanted more. Wanted deeper. If I was going to do anal for the first time, then I was going to make sure that I did it right. I wanted to be fucked. Really fucked. And he was the man to give it to me.

He pulled my hips back sharply, suddenly all the way inside of my ass in one fell swoop – my eyes bugged out for a moment and I let out a cry, but it was pleasure more than pain. He was using the wetness from my last orgasm as all the lubricant that he needed to get me where I needed to go, and it felt so delicious to have him slowly devirginizing my ass like this, in front of all these men.

I glanced to the screen, saw the woman let out a soft moan of delight, and mimicked the noise at once. I could see the men in the dark around me, lit only by the light coming from the screen, as they touched themselves – almost none of them were pretending to do anything other than jerk it right now, stroking themselves to the sight of me like this. I tried to take all of them in, but most of what I could see were just shapes, silhouettes. I didn't need to know who they were or see their faces. I just had to know that they wanted me, that they wanted me more than anything in the world, and that I was going to give that to them every way that they wanted it.

He took his time, sodomizing me, and soon, the feeling of his cock in my ass had started to grow seriously pleasurable. I couldn't help but slip my hand under my pussy and start to play with myself again – even though I just had the most incredible orgasm, I was already hungry for more.

"Yeah, play with yourself while you take my dick in your ass," The man behind me murmured, and he landed a sharp, playful slap on my behind. I moaned loudly, arched my back, and told him to go deeper. I wanted him to really fuck me, really get inside of me and use me the way he wanted to.

And soon, he did. It didn't take long till he was slamming deep inside my ass, his heavy balls slapping up against my pussy roughly as he moved into me over and over again. I rubbed my clit harder, tipping my head back, as he grasped my ass tightly, spreading it open so that he could have easy access to pound me out just like he wanted to.

"Oh, ohhh," I panted, and soon, the intensity of all of this had grown too much – if I had thought the orgasm I'd had the last time had been a lot, it hadn't come close to what I was experiencing now. My pussy was starting to clench, the feeling of his throbbing member inside my ass was building a pleasure that I had never felt before in my life.

When I came, it felt like an explosion, coursing out from between my legs and consuming me from top to bottom. I cried out, so loud that it drowned out the sound of the movie that was still playing in front of us, but I didn't care. All the times that I'd hooked up with people in risky places, knowing that I could have been caught at any instant, it had all come down to this – all built up to this moment, when I could do nothing but let myself get caught up in the thrill of being in public like this and being taken by men I didn't even know.

As soon as I came, the man who was fucking my ass finished, too, like he had just been holding out long enough to make sure that I got to where I needed to be before he took what he had to. He held himself deep inside of me, his cock throbbing deep in my asshole before he pulled out and let me crash down to the velvet seats in front of me.

I turned over, facing the men who were still left. I knew that they were all just waiting for permission, and honestly, I wanted nothing more than to give it to them.

"I need all of you," I moaned to them, loudly enough that they could hear me. And it didn't take long before I had a couple of volunteers step forward and show me just how much they wanted me.

There must have been a couple of dozen men in there in total, and each and every one of them wanted to show me just what a good fuck he was – and God only knew how happy I was to let them do that. I wanted to be used any way that these men saw fit. Some of them focused all on my pleasure – going down on me, sucking and licking at my nipples, massaging my feet – and others seemed more interested in what they could get out of it themselves. They were the ones who fucked me hard and fast, used me just as they wanted to, and God, the thrill of it was enough to set my body on fire.

My pussy was fucked plenty more – that seemed to be the one that most of them wanted to sample and there was no way that I was going to deny a single one of them the pleasure. A few more fucked my mouth, and I enjoyed every moment of tasting their cocks – the big ones, the small ones, the long ones, the short ones, the heavy balls pressing against my tongue so that I had no choice but to worship each and every one. The men changed, the smells and the tastes stayed the same. I just wanted more, more than I could take. I had already reached the very limits of what I knew that I could handle, and I wanted to see where else it could go after this.

And soon, they grew impatient. I didn't mind, not one little bit – no, in fact, as I felt one of them push my pussy down onto his sheathed cock, and another pressing at my asshole, I knew that I couldn't hold back any longer.

I might have liked to think that I could contain myself, but I knew that I couldn't. I wanted to be used and I wanted to be fucked and I wanted them to have me.

The fullness of having two cocks in me at one time was almost more than I could wrap my head around, but I closed my eyes and let it move through me. The thin wall that separated my pussy and my ass was stretched tight, so tight that I could feel the men who were both fucking me right now moving inside of me at the same time. The sheer shock of it, the way that it felt, almost wiped my brain clean of any thoughts at all. How could anything be on my mind when I knew that they were taking me like this? When I knew that I could fit both of these men within me at the same time? How many more could I take, how much more could I handle? I knew that this should have been enough, but honestly, it felt as though I was just starting to understand everything that I could take.

By the time that I had worked my way through all the men in that theater, I was panting hard, soaked in sweat and my own juices, splayed on one of the heavy velvet seats as I caught my breath again. The men around me were spent, and I was proud to say that I had been the one to wring them all dry. I could take all of them, and I could take more on top of that – the girl performing on that big screen, she might have been good, but I knew that I was better.

And, as I smiled up at the dim lights above me, I felt a surge of confidence rush through my body. This was it. This was who I was meant to be – totally unstoppable, totally impossible to hold down. Something more than I had been before.

And something that nobody would be able to take away from me now that I had managed to find it.

Chapter 14

M/F, Vaginal Sex, Cuckold

I eased myself slowly out of the bath, the warm water soothing my lower half a little after the rampant fucking I had taken just a few days before.

Honestly, I was still bathing in the delicious afterglow of everything that I had experienced while I had been in that theater. Honestly, in some ways, it still felt like it couldn't have been more than a fantasy that I was clinging on to – something that I had made up just to put a pin in the delightful sexual awakening that I had been through since I had come to this place and made a new life all of my own here. But I knew from the tenderness in my pussy and my ass that it had been as real as they came.

And that it wouldn't be the last time I would take a fucking like that, if I could help it.

But for now, I needed to rest up, make sure that I didn't get too ahead of myself thinking about what I could do now that I had started to uncover this new side of myself. I was sure that the kink club I had gone to would have plenty more for me to indulge in once I was feeling a little steadier on my feet again, but I was more than happy to relax and enjoy everything that I had taken in these last few months.

And it had all started here. On that very first day, that I had been with the man who had helped me bring my bags in and get unpacked in this new life of mine. Hard to believe that it had really been almost three months ago now – hard to believe that so much had happened that I never could have believed it would before. I had discovered that my sexuality was about as far from straight as I could imagine, shared threesomes, foursomes, more-somes – explored kinks, learned about the power dynamics that turned me on, and discovered how much I could enjoy my own company when it came down to it, too.

I had been so repressed before. I didn't even realize it until I had found a way to break free of everything that had been holding me back, but now, it was as clear as day. I was never going to go back to the person that I was, never going to bother dropping the pretense that I was anything other than the woman I had become. Any person who wanted to be part of my life, they were going to have to accept that I was a full-blown and totally proud slut – a girl who was willing to try anything once. And maybe just a couple more times after that, to make sure. You never know, right?

As I dried myself off with my towel, I heard a buzz at the door – I tucked it around me to cover myself up, and went to answer it.

"Hello?" I spoke into the intercom.

"Hi, sorry to bother you," A male voice came down the line. "I'm here from the moving company. We were clearing out one of our old vans, and we found a box of your stuff that we wanted to drop off. Can I come up?"

"Oh, of course," I replied at once, feeling a happy little flutter in my chest. I had no idea if the man on the other end of the line was the one who had managed to fuck me right the first day that I had moved in here, but damn, I was sincerely willing to try and find out. Would be rude not to, right?

"Thanks."

I buzzed him up, and there was a knock on the door a moment later – I fluffed my hair in the mirror, checking that I at least looked cute, and flashed myself a smile. I knew that it came off me in waves, the kind of woman that I was now, and nobody was going to be able to resist that from me.

I opened the door, put a smile on my face, and greeted the man on the other side – and sure enough, there he was. The very same one that had been there on that first day of my new life. I could hardly believe it, my lips parting with surprise, and I would bet from the way that he was looking at me, too, that he was about as surprised as they came.

"Oh, hey," I greeted him. I wondered if he remembered me. Surely, he didn't just go around fucking every woman that he did a move for, did he? Honestly, I didn't care. If he did, we would have been sluts alike. Maybe that was just one thing we had in common, but it was worth celebrating.

"You want to come in?" I asked him. He was holding a box of stuff in his hands, and I wasn't even sure that I recognized it was mine – it had been so long since I had stuffed all my stuff into boxes and gotten the hell out of my old place that I had forgotten everything that I had packed. I didn't care. As long as it had brought him back to my door, I would take anything that he gave me.

"Thanks for letting me in," he replied, and he slipped past me and into the apartment. God, he smelled good, I had almost forgotten how delicious it was to be around him. There was a reason that he had been the start of all of this for me, and I would always have that to thank him for, wouldn't I?

"And sorry for missing the box the first time around," He continued, as he planted it down on my coffee table.

"Oh, that's okay," I replied. He flicked his gaze back to me, his eyes travelling up and down my body. What he could see of it, hidden under this towel, at least.

"I was a little...distracted," he murmured. I knew what was going through his mind. And there was no way that, even with the tenderness from the gangbang that I'd been a part of, I was going to pass up the chance to do something about it.

"I think I remember that," I replied, playing innocent, even though I was anything but.

"Care to distract me again?" He asked, taking a step towards me. My lips parted into a smile. And I pushed the towel from my shoulders to let him know that he could have me any way he wanted right now.

As soon as the fabric hit the floor, his hands were on me. All over me. Starving for me, like he had been waiting for this since the last time he walked out. His hands sank into my ass, and this time, I made sure that I gave as good as I got, kissing him back, pushing my tongue into his mouth, running my fingers through his hair. I had forgotten how strong and sweet his body was pressed against mine, how deliciously tempting he was, how hard to deny.

I could already feel the hardness of his cock against my hip, and, even though I knew that I probably should have been giving my pussy a break from dick right now, one more wouldn't hurt, right? The way that my pussy was aching at the thought of it told me that she could still handle anything that any man threw at us — after everything that I had been through, everything that I had so deeply enjoyed, all the ways that I had learned that I could pleasure this body of mine, one more dick was going to be just fine.

I guided him through to the bedroom and pulled him down on top of me; he kissed me softly, almost tender, or it would have been if it wasn't for the fact that I was hurriedly undoing his pants as he made out with me. How many men would I have in this bed by the time that I moved out of this place, I wondered — how many would pass through, get to fuck me, get to make me come, and then leave again? I had no clue. I didn't care. I wasn't sure that any number I could have come up with would have been enough...

I reached for a condom in the bedside cabinet and handed it to him once I had pushed his pants down far enough to expose his cock. He didn't need to be told twice. I doubted that he had come to this expecting to get another fuck from me, but he didn't know the woman that I had become since the last time that we had seen one another. I was new now. Different. Different than I had ever been, and I was sure different than I ever would be, the sweet feeling of being in this body, of really owning the way that I felt, the pleasure that I knew I was capable of, was something that I was never going to be able to get over. Not really. And I didn't want to, either. I wanted to stay in this sweet place, this place where I got to enjoy myself and my body and everything that came with living in it no matter what.

I looked down between my legs, pulled my knees back as he pushed into me, watching his cock slowly inch inside my pussy. I wondered if it felt different to him now, after all that I'd done, but judging by the reaction as soon as he thrust into me, it was still just as good as it had ever been – he groaned loudly, took hold of me hard. His hands sank into my body and I could tell that this was everything he had wanted it to be. Had he thought of me in the time that we had been apart? I was sure that he had. Sure that he had fantasized about being with me, about how it would feel to fuck me like this again.

How many fantasies had I filled out, since I had shared myself with so many different lovers over these last few months? I hoped that none of them would forget about me. I hoped that I would linger on in their memories, a part of our time together sticking out for them, no matter what.

The thought of it was enough to make me a little wild with want for this man. I grabbed him, reaching down to sink my fingers into his ass and drive him even deeper inside of me. I wanted to feel him fill me. I wanted to feel that cock of his plunge so deep inside of me it felt as though we would never be able to draw apart, ever again. I could already feel his breath in my ear, the heat of it boiling me from the inside out.

I was grinding myself against him, my clit pressed against his body, and I couldn't get enough of the delicious way that it felt to be with him right now. The sheer power of his cock as it moved into me. How many men had I fucked since the last time I'd seen him? I wished that I could whisper it into his ear, tell him how many guys I'd fucked since him – I bet he'd love it, love to hear the way I had allowed other men to fuck me the way I wanted to be fucked. How many?

"I've fucked so many guys since I last saw you" I breathed in his ear. I could feel his body tensing, but he didn't stop moving inside of me. Surprised, maybe, but not put off.

"How many?"

I didn't know, and yet, I still felt as though his cock was as good and as perfect as it had been the first time. Just went to show, it wasn't about the size or shape of the cock, but the man it was attached to. And what he could do with it...

2 More than I can count, 2 I murmured back, reaching down to grab his back and hold him in place. I looked into his eyes, wanting him to know that he was screwing a woman that he had no control over. That he would never own me – that I would always belong to the other men, the other women who wanted to fuck me.

"Was it good"? He asked. I traced my tongue over his jaw and smiled.

"So good", I moaned.

And that seemed to push him even further over the edge. As though he wanted to prove to me that he was more than some cuckold – that he was more than just another man to me. And this particular man knew just how to get me where I needed to go. I could already feel myself starting to clench, that familiar feeling deep in my stomach telling me that I was getting closer and closer to the edge – I needed this, needed to come, needed one more gift to take me where I had to go before I could relax for the day.

And, sure enough, it didn't take long, just a few more thrusts, before his cock twitched inside of me and he let out a deep growl of pleasure – and I felt my pussy contract around him, tightening to contain him. Once again, it was knowing that I had been enough for him that got me off. Knowing that I was hot enough, sexy enough, desirable enough. That's what I got off on.

We held each other as we came, our bodies wrapped up in each other, both of us focused in on our own pleasure and the way that it seemed to overlap with the other person's. I smoothed his hair gently, feeling almost tender towards this man, this man who had started it all, in the first place. This man who had taken me to places that I had never known I needed to go.

Slowly, he pulled out of me, and he kissed me again, softer this time, lips just skimming against mine. I smiled at him as he pulled back, gazing into his eyes, into the eyes of this man I hardly knew. I hardly needed to know him, either. All that I needed from him was the promise that we had found each other when we had needed each other most – that I had found him when I had been looking for someone to show me the kind of person that I could be.

No matter if we never saw each other again – he would always have a place in my heart. And, of course, in my bed, too.